"I don't want to look at you, or talk to you, either. I'm going back to the party."

"No, you're not. You're going to face me."

Hope had no choice, she told herself as he turned her slowly around. He was her weakness. She had never known anyone like Trace Morgan. Perhaps there *was* no one else like him.

"That's better." He slid one hand up to curve around her throat in a tentative caress. "Listen, Hope. I've done them a favor. They can't lose. If Andy takes the job and Bree can't handle it, they weren't meant to be together. If he turns down the job to make her happy, then…well, that will prove something, too."

"But…"

"If you've got so much faith in them, let them handle this on their own."

"Trace!" She brought her fists down on his chest in a light blow of frustration. "Will you let me get a word in edgewise?"

"No," he said around a smile that was almost a grimace, and kissed her.

Dear Reader,

Help us celebrate life, love and happy-ever-afters with our great new series.

Everybody loves a party, and birthday parties best of all, so join some of your favorite authors and celebrate in style with seven fantastic new romances. One for every day of the week, in fact, and each featuring a truly wonderful woman whose story fits the lines of the old rhyme, "Monday's child is..."

> Monday's child is fair of face,
> Tuesday's child is full of grace,
> Wednesday's child is full of woe,
> Thursday's child has far to go,
> Friday's child is loving and giving,
> Saturday's child works hard for its living,
> And a child that's born on a Sunday,
> Is bonny and blithe and good and gay.

(Anon.)

Does the day on which you're born affect your character? Some people think so—if you want to find out more, read our exciting new series. Available wherever Harlequin books are sold:

Happy reading,

The Editors, Harlequin Romance

A Simple Texas Wedding
Ruth Jean Dale

Harlequin Books

TORONTO • NEW YORK • LONDON
AMSTERDAM • PARIS • SYDNEY • HAMBURG
STOCKHOLM • ATHENS • TOKYO • MILAN
MADRID • WARSAW • BUDAPEST • AUCKLAND

PB
FIC

ISBN 0-373-03424-5

A SIMPLE TEXAS WEDDING

First North American Publication 1996.

CHAPTER ONE

THE legendary Morgan temper was in full flower this blustery March morning.

Although many players in the game of big business and high finance thought it had skipped a generation with Trace Morgan, they simply didn't understand that the brilliant young leader of the Flying M empire had an Achilles heel.

That Achilles heel was family—what little he had left. Although only thirty and rich as Croesus, he knew a great deal about love and loss and he'd had enough.

He'd protect his own, whatever it took. Such were his thoughts as he stomped across the polished hardwood floor and through the open double doors into the dining room of the Flying M Ranch fifty miles southeast of Dallas, Texas. A maid glanced up anxiously from a magnificent antique sideboard where she'd just placed a steaming carafe of coffee. Without waiting to be told, she filled a cup and carried it to him.

"Good mornin', Mr. Morgan," she said, her Texas accent pronounced. "Can I bring your breakfast now?"

"No, you may not." Trace accepted the china cup and saucer with muttered thanks before adding, "Is my sister in her room?"

His glare wasn't meant for the maid, but she was quelled by it just the same. "N-no, sir. You sure you don't want somethin' to eat? Lillian said—"

"Lillian's not the boss here," he said curtly. "When I want something to eat I know how to ask for it."

The maid backed away a few steps, nodded and scurried out of the room. Trace didn't watch her go. He was thinking about his sister, not the help and certainly not food. When he got his hands on Sabrina— He carried his cup to the French doors and stared out moodily.

The Texas landscape wasn't much to look at with a raw March wind whipping past and gray skies overhead. If he wasn't so concerned about his little sister, he'd be tempted to chuck it all and take that vacation he'd been promising himself for the past three years...maybe get in a little skiing in Colorado or even—

"Trace Morgan!"

He turned slowly. "Yes, Lillian?"

The Flying M housekeeper might be sixty-plus and a smidge under five-foot-two, but she had the presence of an Amazon. She also had decades of service, which earned her the right to tell the current head of the Morgan empire exactly what she thought on all subjects.

Which she was not at all shy about doing. "Trace Morgan, what's that supposed to mean—no breakfast? You set yourself down there." She pointed imperiously at the highly polished table and his place, the carved Chippendale armchair at the head. "You better tell me what you want for breakfast or I'll bring you what you ought to have!"

Trace laughed a little ruefully, distracted by her fierceness despite himself. Lillian was truly more like the mother he'd wanted than his real mother had ever been. But then, Hilary Morgan had always had more important things to do than concern herself with her children. That's why she hired nannies—by the handsful, since none of them ever stayed long enough to make a difference.

Trace could understand that. He wouldn't have put up with Hilary, either, if he'd had a choice. Soon enough, he hadn't.

Fortunately, Lillian had taken up the slack. In all his thirty years, Trace couldn't remember a time when she hadn't been nagging him to eat properly, sleep properly, and more recently, marry properly. He tolerated from this little steamroller that which he wouldn't tolerate from another living soul, and for the most part, did so cheerfully.

"I saw that smile. Don't you go laughin' at me, now," she warned. "You know I don't like messin' in your personal life—"

That brought forth *real* laughter, which earned him a full-fledged glare.

"Now, you know I don't," she insisted. "I only do it when you've clearly got the bit in your teeth. Set down here like I told you and I'll have the cook fix those blueberry pancakes you like so much."

"I don't want pancakes, I want Sabrina to—"

"No need to worry about Bree. That nice Archer boy won't let her come to any harm." Lillian planted her hands on her hips and faced him, obviously not the least bit intimidated. "If you don't want pancakes, how about a nice steak with two or three fried eggs?"

"No!" Trace ground his teeth together at her flagrant disregard for his wishes. "It's almost eight o'clock in the morning, and if I could get my hands on that nice Archer boy, I'd wring his neck." He gripped his coffee cup so hard the contents sloshed over the rim. "Dammit, where *is* she?"

"Right here, Trace."

At the sound of his sister's defiant voice, Trace wheeled around. She stood just inside the room, her cheeks rosy with cold and her blue eyes sparkling with challenge.

And something else he didn't want to see—excitement? Trace gritted his teeth. Her hair, as blond as his own was dark, tumbled in disarray around her face and over her shoulders. When she tossed off her full-length leather coat, her clothes looked as if she'd slept in them. Son of a—

"I'd love some breakfast, Lillian," Sabrina announced, dropping the coat over a chair and heading for the sideboard. She helped herself to a cup of coffee and turned with a brilliant smile. "Toast and juice would be fine and...take your time, will you? I need to talk to big brother."

"Him." Lillian sniffed disdainfully. "Be careful. He's grouchy as an ol' bear this morning." She turned toward the door, then hesitated. "We've got some real nice papaya this mornin'. How about that instead of the juice?"

"Fine, Lillian. Thanks."

Trace waited until the housekeeper left the room before rounding on his sister. "What the hell's the meaning of this, Sabrina?" he demanded. "If you intend to stay out all night, the least you can do is let me know. I've been half out of my mind with—"

"I didn't intend it, Trace," she interrupted. "It just happened." With a smile at once hopeful and scared, she thrust out her left hand, fingers spread so he couldn't possibly miss the ring on her third finger.

The *engagement* ring with the tiny diamond. He captured her hand in a grip so harsh it made her gasp, staring down at the ring with something akin to horror.

"Not again," he said flatly.

She yanked her hand away with a familiar flash of temper. "That's not fair," she cried. "This time it's different. I love Andy and he loves me. We're going to be married and there's nothing you can do to stop us."

"Grow up, Sabrina." Trace set his cup and saucer on the table and jammed his hands deep into his pants pockets. He had to, to keep from grabbing her and shaking her until her teeth rattled. "This is your third engagement ring ... or is it the fourth? I've lost count."

Sabrina thrust out her lower lip and glared at him. "Those weren't engagement rings, they were *friendship* rings ... well, all except one. Or maybe two—anyway, this is different. Andy's not like any of the other guys I've dated. He's ..."

She got a sappy, faraway look on her face that made her brother want to turn her over his knee. Andrew Archer wasn't all that different, no matter what she professed to believe, Trace thought cynically. Two of her previous loves had been boys she'd grown up with, and Trace had never taken them seriously. But one had been a kid like Andy, an opportunist from the wrong side of the tracks who was interested in the heiress, not the beautiful, headstrong girl longing for love. He hadn't fooled Trace, though. A subtle word, a hefty check, and he was out of her life for good.

"Sabrina," he began in a warning tone.

Quick tears filled her eyes, to his utter astonishment. His sister never cried, she *fought*. Part of being a Morgan was being tough.

She didn't look tough at the moment. "Please, Trace, don't ruin this," she begged. "Give us a chance."

"Us?" Trace looked past her with exaggerated curiosity. "Now that you bring it up, where is this paragon of virtue? Why is he letting you take the rap all by yourself? Surely he's aware that as head of the Morgan family, I'll have a lot of questions about this sudden engagement."

She seemed to find her fighting spirit and lifted her chin, defiant once more. "He wanted to be with me when I told you but I begged him to let me handle it. I knew how you'd react."

"Honey, anyone who loves you would react the same way. Hell, you've only been dating this clown for a few months."

"What difference does that make? It was love at first sight."

"There's no such thing as love at first sight."

He expected anger. Instead she gave him a glance filled with pity. "Sometimes I think you don't believe in love at all, at first sight or any sight," she whispered.

Her attitude and expression irritated the hell out
of him. It was almost like being lectured—by his
little sister? Not very damned likely.

"Sure I do," he said sharply. What did she think
he was, a robot? Okay, maybe he'd never been in
love, but he'd sure fallen into lust a time or two.
"Love doesn't strike like a lightning bolt," he
argued. "Love—the real kind, anyway, as opposed
to simple passion—takes time. And if it's going to
have a snowball's chance in hell of lasting, it better
be with someone who shares a similar background
and values."

"Stick to my own kind, is that what you're
saying?" Her voice rose.

"Yeah, I am. This Andy... He's from a poor
family, if I recall."

"Practically everybody's poor by your stan-
dards, Trace." She refilled her coffee cup. "You're
a snob."

"I'm realistic."

"So am I. I don't care about the money or the
social position."

"You would if you didn't have them."

"Are you talking about me or...Rebecca?"

They stood in shared, if silent, sorrow for a few
moments. Then he said caustically, "Yes, I guess
I was thinking of her. I wonder why."

A red tide washed over Sabrina's cheeks. "I'm
not Rebecca, and Andy's not after my money, or
yours, either. When you get to know him, you'll
see I'm right."

"I suppose anything's possible." He forced
himself to say words he didn't believe because he

loved her, but honesty made him add in grim warning, "But don't count on it."

"I *am* counting on it." She set her cup and saucer on the sideboard. Turning, she threw her arms around her brother's neck. "Trace," she whispered in a voice that trembled, "you're the only really close family I have left. I love you, and I want you to love my husband—and that's going to be Andrew Archer. Please, please give us a chance."

He wished he could offer the assurance she sought. But the truth of the matter was, he had no intention of standing by and letting her ruin her life by marrying some yahoo from the wrong side of the tracks who was doubtless after her for all the wrong reasons. If she thought he was, she had another think coming.

As head of the Morgan family and fortune, Trace Morgan would leave no stone unturned to make his headstrong sister see things the right way—his way. But he'd try to achieve that without alienating her for all time.

He loved her more than anyone in the world. All he wanted was her happiness.

"A chance isn't that much to ask," he said slowly, kissing the top of her head before setting her away. "You've just surprised me, Sabrina." *Shock's more like it.* "I had no idea you were serious about this guy or I'd have paid more attention. Now which one is he? His parents—"

"His father died years ago and his mother more recently. He was raised right here in Dallas."

She seemed happy to accept her brother's words at face value, without delving beneath the surface. "He doesn't have any brothers or sisters but he grew up with a cousin who's his age—he's twenty-five. Her name's Hope and she's like a sister to him. I think you'll like her, Trace, although she's definitely not your type."

"My *type*?" He laughed incredulously. "What type is that?"

"Sophisticated long-legged blondes with expensive tastes." She shrugged. "Hope's about my size, actually—five-four or five. She's one of the sweetest people I've ever known, as well as the most generous—generous with herself, if you know what I mean. If you ever need a favor, Hope's the one to turn to. She always comes through. Andy told me they used to joke about it when they were kids— Hope is a true Friday's child...so loving and giving."

Damning with faint praise, Trace thought. He didn't care about somebody's *cousin*. He cut straight to the chase. "Tell me more about Andy. What does he do that will support you in the style to which you're accustomed?"

She made a face at him. "He's an environmental engineer and a lot more worried about supporting me in style than I am. He's also the kindest, most thoughtful, most romantic man I ever—"

She prattled on happily while Lillian served their breakfast with many nods of approval. Trace managed to smile, ask polite questions and keep his reservations to himself.

But that didn't mean he'd resolved any of his familial concerns. Family was more important to him than anything in the world. Since all he had left was Sabrina, that meant she was the lucky, if unwilling, target of all that concern.

One thing was sure—whatever he did, it would be for her own good.

Hope Archer threw her arms around her cousin's neck and gave him a delighted hug. "Congratulations, Andy, I'm so happy for you! Where's Sabrina? Why isn't she here so I can welcome her to the family?"

Andy returned her hug, then gave her a lopsided smile. "She's home, breaking the news to her brother." He grimaced.

"Surely you don't anticipate any problems from that quarter. Who wouldn't be thrilled to have *you* in their family?"

Andy chuckled at her enthusiasm, but beneath his happiness about the engagement, he looked tired and a little apprehensive.

"What is it?" she asked with quick concern. "Is there a problem?"

"Could be." He ran a hand absently through his brown hair, glancing around the shop.

Hope's heart went out to him. Automatically, he was looking for his mother. Celebrations had been Aunt Ellen's party-planning business, her livelihood and her joy, but he wasn't going to find her here today amidst the balloons and the favors and the foliage and the wicker furnishings. Ellen Archer had died last summer in a boating accident, and neither Andy nor Hope had completely adjusted to life without her.

"If I ever needed Mom, now's the time," he said plaintively.

There *was* a problem. Hope touched his elbow lightly. "I'm a poor substitute but I'm at your service. Come on back into the office where we can talk. Mrs. Casen can handle the phone and any walk-ins.''

Mrs. Casen, anybody's perfect image of a grandmother with her white hair and her brown eyes bright behind granny glasses, glanced up from an order sheet, pencil poised. "By all means," she said. "Shouldn't be a problem, no more business than we've had of late.''

"Business bad?" Andy inquired, following Hope toward the back.

She shrugged, making light of a problem that plagued her constantly. "It could be better, but then, could Mrs. Casen and I handle it if it were? Things'll even out, don't you worry.''

They passed through the fabric curtain separating the public from the private areas of the shop. She gestured toward a small round table with two wicker chairs drawn up to it. "Have a seat and I'll get you a cup of tea.''

"Thanks." He slumped into a chair and promptly yawned. "I'm beat. Bree and I were up all night long talking about this, or arguing about it, to be more accurate.''

"Oh?" Puzzled, Hope placed a mug of hot water before him and plopped in a tea bag. "I take it you proposed last night. Did you have to talk her into it?" She ruffled his hair affectionately, earning a rueful chuckle.

"Not exactly." He swished the tea bag around in the mug. "She proposed to me—and had to talk *me* into it.''

"No!" Hope sat opposite him. She laughed uncertainly. "Don't you lov—I mean, I *know* you love her. What's going on, Andy?"

He sipped his tea, taking his time, answering finally like a typical engineer—carefully. "I love her," he said in a voice that left no room for doubt. "She loves me, too. But there are . . . problems."

Hope waved his worries aside. "Life's full of problems. If you love each other, how important can they be?"

"We'll find out, sooner or later. I don't doubt we'll get through this, but it may be rocky for a while."

"So tell me, already." She leaned forward, eager to offer moral support.

"It's her brother."

"Her brother? Usually it's parents."

"Her parents are dead. Her brother, Trace, is head of the family empire."

Hope raised a brow. "Empire? I knew her family must be well-off the minute I saw her. She's got that *expensive* look about her, if you know what I mean."

"I don't. If I had, we'd probably never have gotten involved."

"What a snobbish attitude! I'm surprised at you, Andrew Archer, intimidated by a little money."

"Look," he said impatiently, "we're not talking about a *little* money. We're talking about a damned fortune. Did you ever hear of the Flying M?"

"Flying M Enterprises? Flying M Bank? Flying M Ranch? Who in Texas hasn't heard of the Flying M?" Her eyes widened. "No! You don't mean—"

"I wish I didn't. The M stands for Morgan. Bree's great-grandpa started the whole thing about a hundred years ago and every Morgan since has added to the pie. When her father died a few years ago, her brother, Trace Morgan, took over everything—including her."

"Oh, dear." Hope tried to take it all in. Great wealth was not something with which she had personal experience. But then, money was never a real issue. "Do you mean her brother doesn't like you?"

"Like me? He doesn't know me. We've only met a couple of times, and that very briefly."

"Then . . . I don't understand."

Andy looked disconsolate. "It's like this. Bree's brother has made mincemeat out of every guy she ever got even halfway serious about. So she never let on to him that we were getting . . . close."

"I see." She frowned, trying to reason this out. "Since their father's dead, perhaps her brother just takes his responsibilities very seriously," Hope suggested softly, trying to put the best interpretation on what he had told her.

"Yeah, right." Andy looked and sounded dubious. "The truth is, if I'd known who she was— who her family was—I doubt I'd ever have asked her out in the first place. But once I did, I was a goner."

Hope's romantic heart melted. She'd thought from the moment she met Bree that this was the woman for the cousin she loved like a brother. Now curiosity got the better of her. "Did she really propose to you?"

"She sure did, but that was a mere formality. I had an engagement ring in my pocket, so she didn't exactly take me by surprise. Then we spent the rest of the night trying to figure out how to tell her brother. She finally convinced me that it was better to let her do it alone, but damn! I feel rotten about it. Like a shirker, somehow.''

He looked so thoroughly miserable that Hope felt her throat tighten with sympathy. If there was one thing Andy *wasn't*, it was a shirker. ''It'll be all right,'' she assured him. ''I know it will.''

He managed a grin. ''True love conquers all, huh? I sure hope you're right.'' He squared his shoulders as if throwing off his cares. ''So—how's the party-planning business, really?''

''A little slow.''

An understatement, if there ever was one. Since Aunt Ellen's death, business had fallen off by at least half. Although Hope had quit her job with an employment agency and stepped in at once to help out, she'd barely been able to keep Celebrations afloat.

She'd just have to try harder. She knew how much profit the business had to make each month in order to stay afloat—and she had to stay afloat, no matter what! She'd gone out on a limb to keep the business in the family after her aunt's death, for sentimental reasons at first. But she'd since discovered that she, too, loved making people happy by finding ways to lift their special occasions out of the ordinary.

Of course, Aunt Ellen had done it better, but Ellen had been a very special woman. A widow, she hadn't thought twice about taking in her orphaned niece and raising her right along with her own son, Andy. And she'd hung onto her dreams, saving money from her job as a legal secretary to start Celebrations. Once she'd opened her doors, success was guaranteed.

Ellen was a born hostess and party planner, so good at it, in fact, that business boomed. She'd handled it all with aplomb. Not only did she plan and supervise the events for which she was paid, she also pitched in for those who couldn't possibly afford her services. The beneficiaries of this generosity would never know it, though, because the bills they got were a mere pittance compared to what Ellen actually spent to give them memories to last a lifetime.

Hope wanted nothing more than to carry on in that family tradition, but it wasn't always easy. She'd taken Celebrations on almost on a whim. What she knew about throwing parties you could put in your eye and never even blink. Her idea of a party was a roomful of pleasant people, a box of crackers, a chunk of cheese and a couple of bottles of wine.

But it hadn't taken her long to realize that she, like her beloved aunt, had found her niche, a way to make a living while making people happy at the same time. And also like her aunt, Hope didn't have it in her to turn down a neighborhood kid who'd ask with big, soulful eyes what it would cost to have a clown at his birthday party, or an eighty-plus-year-old man who longed to throw a real wingding for his beloved wife to celebrate their sixtieth wedding anniversary.

Fortunately, Hope was a fast learner. It took all her time and effort, but hard work didn't frighten her. With Mrs. Casen's help, Hope was somehow muddling through.

Of course, if they got anything more complicated than the usual—children's birthdays and wedding anniversaries—she'd be in big trouble.

Now Hope sighed and said to her favorite cousin, "Enough about business. Tell me what Bree's brother could possibly do to mess things up."

"Who knows? She's afraid he'll find some way to pull the rug out from under us. We want his blessing and if we can't get it . . . well, it'd break Bree's heart." He shrugged as if to hide his own concern. "We're hoping that when he sees how things are with us, he'll come around. But from what she says, that may not happen."

Hope caught her breath in alarm. "What will you do if he doesn't?"

"I'm . . . not sure. Family means a lot to both of us and I wouldn't want to deprive Bree of hers. But we love each other, dammit, and we won't let anyone or anything come between us."

Swallowing sympathetic tears, Hope nodded. "If you love each other, nothing *can* come between you," she declared staunchly. "Let's assume the best, not the worst. Let's assume that Mr. Morgan will realize you're the only man in the world who can make his sister happy. In that case, what kind of wedding do the two of you want?"

"Simple," Andy said decisively. "Simple and quick, just the two of us and our immediate families and a few very special friends. Bree's godfather is a judge and she'd like him to perform the ceremony."

"What about a reception?"

Andy chuckled. "We talked about that. Throw a few buckets of buffalo wings on the table, break out a case of beer for toasts and call it done."

He looked so pleased with himself that Hope burst out laughing. He—the son of a professional party planner, about to marry the daughter of one of the most socially prominent families in Dallas—thought he could get away with a simple little ol' wedding, did he?

Sure, Andy, she thought. In your dreams!

Andy had been gone for less than an hour when the bell above the front door of Celebrations announced a new arrival—Sabrina. Delighted, Hope rushed to embrace the young woman her cousin loved.

But Sabrina trembled in Hope's embrace. Hope drew back, alarmed. "What in the world is the matter?"

"Nothing." Bree looked uncomfortable saying it. "Is Andy here?"

"I'm sorry, you just missed him. Would you like me to call his office to see if he's come in?"

"No, no. Actually—" Bree let out her breath on a note of relief "—I really need to talk to you. Is this a good time?"

"Perfect." Taking Bree's hand, Hope drew her toward the office, where she'd earlier had tea with Andy. "Honey, I can't tell you how thrilled I am by the news."

Bree's smile was brilliant. "Thanks—I need to hear that. I just told my brother and believe me, I can use a little reinforcement about now."

"Then you've come to the right place," Hope declared staunchly. "Can I offer you a cup of tea?"

"No, thanks. No tea, just sympathy, a friendly ear and a little advice."

Hope laughed. "Both my ears are friendly, but my advice—" She shook her head. "I'm not so sure about that."

"I am." Bree seemed to be relaxing a bit. "I need to talk to you about my brother."

"Well, of course. Andy's mentioned your... concerns. But I don't know how much help I can be, since I've never met him."

"That's okay," Bree said. "I'll tell you all you need to know."

Hope had to admit she was curious, so she leaned forward in her chair and waited.

Bree seemed to consider her words carefully. "Well, Trace is—please understand, I love him to death. He's my only close remaining relative. I adore him."

"I'll try to remember that."

"Good. Well, Trace is smart and handsome as the devil and everything he touches turns to money, which I guess is good." Bree bit her lip, then burst out, "He's also arrogant and pigheaded and bossy. As far as he's concerned, I'm still a baby! Just because he's so much older than I am—"

Good grief, Hope thought in alarm, Bree's twenty-two, so how old is this ogre of a brother, anyway? Forty?

"—and because he's been the head of the family since Daddy died, he thinks I should jump when he tells me to, or in this case, *not* jump. But I'm grown up. I've got a college degree, I've got a job.

Okay, teaching first graders may not impress a big business tycoon but it keeps me off the streets.''

Hope, who considered teaching a noble calling, was incensed on Bree's behalf. Her brother must be a monster! On the other hand . . . ''Surely you're mistaken,'' she suggested. ''Who wouldn't be proud of a sister dedicated to molding all those innocent little minds? I think teaching is a wonderful profession!''

''Tell that to Trace,'' Bree said glumly.

''Maybe I will. Which reminds me, it's traditional for the bridegroom's family to make the first overture—'' a fact she hadn't known until she read it a few days ago in a wedding checklist she'd found in her aunt's planning book ''—and since I'm the closest family Andy has left, perhaps you'd like me to make the first move.''

Bree shook her head vigorously. ''Please don't. Let me work on Trace a bit more, try to soften him up. I'll get back to you.'' She bit her lip, her lovely face flushing. ''He'd better come around,'' she added grimly, ''because if he doesn't I swear we'll elope! I'm not going to let him browbeat or badger me into giving up the man I love just because—''

Hope watched Bree chew on her lower lip and blink back tears. Patting Bree's hand, Hope made soothing little noises. ''Give your brother time to get used to the idea,'' she urged. ''I'm sure he loves you as much as you love him, Bree. All he wants is for you to be happy.''

Bree sniffled. ''I suppose,'' she said a bit petulantly. ''Well, I'm going to be Mrs. Andrew Archer and Trace can like it or lump it! And I'm not going to wait around forever for my big brother's approval, either."

"No, of course not. But give him a little time to get to know Andy as we do. You don't want to have to choose between the two most important men in your life. And you won't have to, once your brother sees what a great guy Andy is."

Bree looked up with tear-bright eyes. "D-do you really think so?"

"I'm sure of it," Hope declared, believing every word. "I don't know your brother but I know you. You're wonderful, so how bad can *he* be?"

"Yeah . . . how bad?" Bree echoed, but without noticeable confidence.

CHAPTER TWO

HOPE removed a Mylar balloon from the helium tank and clipped the neck. One down and another forty or so to go to the Butlers' fiftieth wedding anniversary. Anticipating how surprised and happy Mrs. Butler would be brought a smile to Hope's lips. She brushed aside the fact that Mr. Butler could only afford to pay about half what such a party would normally cost. She'd make up the difference somehow.

A crack of thunder wiped away her smile and brought her head swinging up in alarm. Through the lettering on the front window of Celebrations, she watched rain pelt down and bounce on sidewalk and walkway. Wouldn't be many people coming into the shop in this weather.

But even as she thought that, a car glided to a stop at the curb—and what a car. Hope had never seen such a vehicle, so long and low and racy. And expensive. That black sports car was probably worth more than her business.

Mrs. Casen hung up the telephone behind the counter and glanced at her young boss. "If it's not one thing, it's another," she announced.

Hope picked up another balloon. "No luck with the suppliers?"

"None whatsoever. We can't get heliotrope and that's that. Mrs. McManus will just have to settle for Heavenly Blue."

"Oh, dear. She's not going to like that."

Mrs. Casen harrumphed. "No, but if I drive over there myself and jolly her along, she'll come around." She headed toward the coatrack at the back of the shop.

Hope frowned. "I don't like you going out in this weather, Mrs. Casen. Why don't I—"

"She won't listen to you." Mrs. Casen shrugged into a shiny red slicker and reached for her umbrella. "I'm sorry, dear, but you know it's true. She thinks you're much too young to handle anything as important as a tea for the new minister. She's quite wrong, of course, and I told her so in no uncertain terms, but—"

"Oh, dear." Mrs. McManus might be picky but she was one of the steadiest clients Celebrations had. If she just wasn't so darned stubborn!

"I've known Jayne McManus for fifty years and she won't pull any of her shenanigans on *me*. It'll be all right. Don't you worry a minute about losing her business."

"If you say so. But I'm still worried about you going out in this rain," Hope said. "Are you sure?"

"Quite sure. It's only a couple of miles and I'll avoid main roads where the traffic may be bad." She blew her employer a kiss. "I'll be back as soon as I can but don't expect me till you see me coming—you know how she is."

Hope certainly did. As Mrs. Casen went out the back, the bell over the front door announced a new arrival. It was Erlene Jones, nervous thirty-something third-time bride-to-be, dashing in out of the rain.

Behind her, Hope noticed the sports car still at the curb. Curious. The driver must be lost or seriously confused.

"Quick!" Erlene shouted, tossing off her dripping hat and coat and sending a spray of droplets spiraling around the room. "I've made up my mind! Get your books before I change it again!"

Hope rushed to comply. Erlene's was the first wedding she'd attempted, but if they were all this difficult, Hope wasn't sure she wanted any more.

But even as she hauled sample books and brochures and order forms onto the counter, she glanced again through the window at the mechanical marvel at her curb. Certainly her usual customers in this solidly middle-class neighborhood didn't drive cars like that. In her world, *nobody* did.

But *he* would—the man who walked through the door at that very moment. He had to be the owner of that car, she realized, staring at the tall, broad-shouldered figure half-concealed behind the frenetic bride-to-be. A tentative smile curved her lips.

Then he stepped forward and she saw him. Her smile slipped away as her mouth fell open. She had never seen such a drop-dead-gorgeous man in her life, not even in the movies. He brought with him a presence that filled the small shop and made her heart stop beating.

She guessed him to be about thirty, with dark, almost black hair clipped stylishly close to a well-shaped head. His nose and jawline were strong to the point of forbidding, the effect softened by a sexy cleft in his chin. Except for a certain caution, his face betrayed no real emotion . . . but his eyes did, blue eyes with an alert brilliance that sent a slight shiver of anticipation down her spine.

Erlene gave Hope's elbow a tug. "Did you hear what I said? I'm going with the strapless white lace hoop skirt, the one with all those ruffled tiers, remember? And for my bridesmaids—well, I just couldn't choose between the lime green and the orange so I want both, three bridesmaids in each. I mean, lime and orange are both citrus, right?"

The man had wandered to a children's birthday display and was feigning interest. Hope felt sure he was actually listening to the babbling bride. She swallowed hard and tried to concentrate on Erlene.

"Uh...are you really sure you want to—"

"Don't confuse me! Just write everything down." Erlene pointed to the notepad. "We're all going to wear those little granny boots. You know, the kind that lace over the ankle? White for me and dyed-to-match for them. And net stockings—"

"Net stockings! Don't you think that might be a touch—"

"Don't you get it? This is a theme wedding!"

"It...is?" Hope swallowed hard, fighting to conceal her dismay from the bride, whose feelings she wouldn't hurt for the world. Was that suppressed laughter curving the stranger's bold mouth? "And the theme is...?"

"Old-fashioned. I want everything to be old-fashioned. I want my veil attached to a crown, like Queen Victoria, get it? Old-fashioned? And I want Stacee dressed like Shirley Temple, with those long curls and all, and throw orchid petals."

Stacee the flower girl was the bride's twelve-year-old, five-foot-five-inch-tall daughter.

Shirley Temple?

Erlene rushed on. "I want Franklyn to wear one of them black gambler-type suits, you know, with the white shirt and the little string tie. Do you think it would be too much if he wore a couple of six-guns? You do? Okay, no six-guns. We want this to be in good taste. I settled for second best the first two times I got married but this time it's first class all the way."

Hope tried to concentrate while Erlene expounded on her vision of the perfect wedding. It was hard, though, with that gorgeous man lurking around in the background. What could he want here? Surely not to hire her to plan an event. The very thought made Hope bite her lip to suppress hysterical giggles.

Here she was, trying to guide Erlene toward moderation—a task requiring total concentration—with half her mind following every move the handsome stranger made.

Erlene paused for breath. "Got all that, Hope?"

Hope scrawled a final notation. "Got it, Erlene. But don't you think—"

"No time to think! I'm on my lunch hour and I gotta get back to work. Let me know if you run into any problems." She hugged her consultant and whirled so quickly that she nearly ran into the man loitering behind her. With an appreciative "Excuse me!" she donned hat and coat and flung herself through the door and into the rain at a dead run.

Hope was alone with...him. She dredged up a tentative smile. "Uh...hello. I—I'm...that is..." She swallowed hard and tried to pull her wits together. "I'm..."

He smiled, revealing perfect white teeth. Even his clothes were perfect, from his pale blue rain-repellent jacket all the way down to the toes of his leather athletic shoes, everything expensive yet understated. In short, the man reeked class. He said in a low, sexy voice, "Hope Archer, I presume."

"T-that's right. We haven't met, have we?" Ha! As if she'd forget!

"No, but I've heard all about you, Friday's Child. Your reputation has gone before you."

Before he could say any more, the small bell over the front door jangled open. Hope jumped guiltily, roused from further contemplation of the outrageously attractive individual before her.

Andy barged through the front door with Bree, looking a bit wild-eyed, beside him. When he saw Hope, he let out his breath on a note of relief. "What's been going on here?" he demanded. "We've been calling and calling and your line's been busy for hours."

"Yes." Hope frowned. "We had several calls from people who would've come in except for the weather, and then Mrs. Casen was calling our distributors trying to find—"

Without hesitation, Bree rushed right up to the handsome stranger. "Trace!" she exclaimed. "You're not supposed to meet us here for another half-hour!"

Dazed, Hope looked around helplessly. *This was Trace Morgan*? "Oh, dear," she said weakly. "Oh, dear!"

Bree smiled uncertainly. "I take it you two have met?" She took her brother's hand and drew him forward with a disappointed glance, which included them all. "I wanted to be the one to introduce two of my favorite people—make sure you got off on the right foot and all that."

The smile Trace gave his sister was considerably more genuine than the one Hope had seen from him earlier. "To tell you the truth, we haven't exactly met." Those brilliant eyes singed Hope with blue fire. "I'm Sabrina's wicked older brother," he said.

"I'm Andy's cousin, Hope," she admitted breathlessly.

"I'd know you anywhere," he said, "from Sabrina's description, of course."

She put out her hand. When he hesitated, she withdrew her offer just as he extended his hand. Their glances locked and both laughed, she nervously, he confidently. When his strong hand at last enveloped her smaller one, the contact sent an electric shock all the way up her arm.

She gasped and snatched her hand away, rubbing her palm on her skirt. She rushed into speech. "I'm sorry I was busy when you arrived. If I'd known you were coming—"

"As Sabrina said, I was early. Besides, I rather enjoyed . . . seeing you in action." His glance went past her to settle on his sister's intended, his expression hardening almost imperceptibly. "Andy." Again a handshake, but this one brusque and quick.

Hope glanced from one man to the other, looking for signs of agreement and seeing none. This might turn out to be more of a problem than she'd first thought.

Andy turned to Hope. "Bree and I asked Trace to meet us here thinking we could kidnap you for a little lunch and conversation. Didn't mean to surprise you this way."

"You surprised me, all right." Or *somebody* did.

Bree slipped an arm around Andy's waist, a loving and familiar gesture. "So can you join us for a little wedding talk?" she urged Hope. "Since you're Andy's closest relative, we're counting on you to represent the Archer point of view."

"I'll be happy to do anything I can," Hope agreed, "but we've got a little problem. Mrs. Casen is out at the moment and I'm not sure when—"

"No, dear, I'm back." Mrs. Casen bustled through the curtain between the office and the public area of the shop, leaving puddles on the floor. "And, I might add, all is well." She winked and went about removing her coat. "You run along. Jayne gave me tea and some of those awful poppy seed cookies she's so fond of so I won't want lunch for hours."

"All right." Hope nodded. "I just have to put away this mess on the counter, grab my coat and I'll be right with you, Bree."

"With me," Trace corrected. To Bree and Andy he added, "You two go on. Hope and I will be right behind you." It sounded very much like an order.

Before Hope could protest, it was all settled. Not that the plan entirely lacked appeal . . .

His sports car was almost as powerful and impressive as the man himself—almost but not quite. Absently Hope slid her palm across the leather bucket seat. When Trace gave her an amused glance, she smiled sheepishly, feeling like a country bumpkin.

"I've never been in a car like this before," she admitted candidly. "It's very...nice." She could have said *intimidating* but she didn't.

He drove exactly the way she knew he would, with complete control and utter disregard for speed limits. The rain had stopped and he'd slipped on a pair of aviator sunglasses, making it even more difficult for her to gauge his expression.

He halted the car at a red traffic signal. "So were you surprised when you heard about the engagement?" he asked too casually.

"Yes," she replied with complete honesty, "and no. I knew they were perfect together from the very beginning but I thought it'd take them a lot longer to realize it themselves." When he didn't respond, she added rather tentatively, "You should be pleased that your sister's fallen in love with such a wonderful man."

"Pleased...may be a bit of an overstatement." He guided the car into the restaurant parking lot. Nearby, Andy and Bree were climbing out of his sedan. "She's only twenty-two," Trace continued. "And they haven't known each other very long."

"Long enough to be sure it's the real thing," she said. "Sometimes it doesn't take long."

"That's right, love at first sight. Sabrina's already given me that lecture."

His cool tone cut her to the quick. "I wouldn't presume to give you a lecture," she said stiffly. "But now that you bring it up—yes, I'm talking about love at first sight. Bree and I agree on that point, among others."

"I stand corrected."

Was he angry with her? He removed the key from the ignition and shifted around, reaching up to whip off the dark glasses. He was laughing! Flustered, she fumbled blindly behind her for the door handle, incapable of looking away from those mesmerizing blue eyes.

"Hold it!" he commanded. "Let me."

He was out of the car and around to open her door before she could pull her wits together. He helped her out of the low-slung vehicle with a flourish, then took her elbow lightly to steer her to the couple waiting on the sidewalk.

And as they hung up their coats inside and followed the waiter to their table, Hope puzzled over the few words they'd exchanged in the car. One conclusion seemed inevitable—Trace Morgan was not reconciled to this marriage.

What was he prepared to do to prevent it?

Over coffee, they got down to brass tacks.

"We want a simple ceremony," Bree said. "Just family and a few friends, maybe a small reception afterward. And soon. We don't see any reason to wait."

Trace stirred his coffee, his expression giving nothing away. Suddenly he glanced up, his gaze on Andy intense. "I take it she's speaking for you, as well."

Andy didn't respond to the implied criticism. "I want to marry her, the sooner the better. I don't care if it's in a cathedral or a judge's chambers or city hall. Weddings are for women."

"And honeymoons are for men," Trace suggested, his gaze narrowing.

"Don't be a chauvinist," Bree snapped. "We're trying to be nice about this, big brother, but our plans don't depend on *you*." She waited a few seconds for him to reply. When he didn't, she added cautiously, "What *do* you want?"

"The same thing you're going to want, once you get down off your high horse and think about this logically."

"Which is?"

"Sabrina, you've got friends and family from one side of this state to the other—hell, from one side of this *country* to the other. I've got business associates, then there's all of Dad's friends and past associates—Mother's friends and charity co-workers, and that's only our side of the family."

Bree thrust out her bottom lip. "But I don't care if—"

"Oh, don't you? You just want to sneak away as if you had something to hide, as if you were ashamed—"

"Damn you, Trace!" Face flushed, Bree leaned forward. "How dare you!"

Andy covered her clenched fist with his hand. "Easy, Bree."

To someone who didn't know him as well as Hope did, he probably looked in perfect control.

He wasn't. While Hope cast about for some way to ease the tension, Sabrina threw down yet another gauntlet.

"We're going to do this our way, Trace," she warned. "Don't mess with us or we'll simply elope.

I don't think you'd like that very much, would you?''

Trace went still, and Hope could see that for the first time, he was shaken. She watched him with sympathy. His doubts about this engagement might be wrong, but he obviously loved his sister very much and was simply trying to look out for her interests. He wasn't saying Bree and Andy shouldn't get married, Hope rationalized. He was simply saying that he'd like to make it a more elaborate social occasion than they'd envisioned.

"Hey," she inserted into the tense silence, "we're all friends here. Let's lighten up. Bree, there's plenty of time to plan just the kind of wedding you want—''

"Something simple," Bree said from between clenched teeth.

"Whatever. And Trace, I'm sure she was teasing about eloping. Why, I'd never forgive my favorite cousin if he didn't let me bawl my eyes out at his wedding.''

Andy shot her a grateful glance and Bree managed a weak smile, although it looked a bit grim around the edges. Trace leaned back in his chair, his mouth twisting down in a cynical grimace. Even in that relaxed position, he reminded Hope of a coiled spring.

"There," she declared with relief, "that's better. Now, since I was invited to represent Andy's side of the family, may I propose a toast to the perfect couple?" She lifted her coffee cup and the others did likewise, although in Trace's case, slowly.

"To Sabrina and Andrew," she said, her heart swelling with love...and perhaps just a bit of envy.

Sabrina didn't appear to realize how lucky she was. "The wedding isn't important, but the marriage is. Long life and much happiness."

"Long life," Trace echoed.

They all drank.

Hope dabbed at her damp eyes with the corner of her napkin. "I'm sorry," she apologized. "I'm such a wimp about things like weddings and babies and true love. My sobs will probably drown out the ceremony. Maybe you better make me sit in the back." She gave Andy and Bree an apologetic smile.

"I've got a better idea," Trace said, his tone light but edged with steel. "Why don't we put this whole thing off until Hope thinks she can handle it—say, five or six years?" He looked directly at Andy. "I've got a blank check that says you can find happiness without making your favorite cousin miserable."

For a paralyzed moment, no one moved. Then Sabrina lunged to her feet. Leaning across the table until her face was only inches from her brother's, she glared into his eyes. "How dare you!" she cried.

Andy grabbed her by the waist and pulled her into her chair, although she struggled. Hope stared at Trace, aghast yet half-convinced she'd misunderstood.

Surely he hadn't just offered to buy Andy off! That would be a mean, despicable, unforgivable thing to—

Andy laughed. His face was a little flushed but he spoke with perfect calm. "My favorite cousin loves a good cry," he told Trace, "and I wouldn't dream of depriving her." He stood up, pulling a sputtering Sabrina tight to his side. "And on that happy note, I think we'll take our leave. You will see that Hope gets back to Celebrations?''

"Of course.''

Hope heard frustration in Trace's growl of consent.

"In that case, we're out of here.'' Andy dragged a fuming Sabrina from the room.

Hope looked blankly at Trace. "Why?'' she asked plaintively. "Why did you do that? You've upset Bree terribly—and you haven't done the rest of us much good, either!''

Trace's pleasant facade seemed completely swept aside. "Give your cousin a message for me,'' he said curtly. "Tell him elopement is out. If he insists on marrying my sister, he'll do it the right way—standing up like a man in front of God and everybody.''

"I wouldn't insult Andy by repeating that,'' Hope declared, deeply offended on her cousin's behalf. "He would never elope. Why...why, that would be running away, like he had something to hide. Andy's not like that.''

"Yeah, sure.''

She could see Trace wasn't reassured but she didn't know what else she could say to put his mind at ease. He paid the lunch check and drove her to Celebrations with a minimum of conversation. When he walked her to the door, she turned to him dutifully.

"Thank you for a lovely time,'' she said, out of politeness but meaning it, too. It had been lovely just being with him...for the most part.

He stared down at her with a peculiar, disbelieving expression on his face. "Hope Archer,'' he said at last, a smile tugging at his lips, "are you for real? Or have you truly stepped out of that famous children's rhyme—Friday's Child?"

It took a couple of days—and a lot of fast talking on Hope's part—to get Sabrina to calm down. Andy was no help, since he considered the entire incident over and done with. He simply refused to rehash it.

"It's only an insult if I want to take it that way, and I don't," he said. "The subject is closed."

Maybe for him. It sure wasn't for Sabrina, and she turned to Hope for comfort and support.

"Trace treats me like such a baby," she lamented. "Why is it so hard for him to believe that an honest, smart, handsome, ethical, *wonderful* man like Andy could love me?"

Hope gave her future cousin-in-law a sympathetic hug. "I don't think that's it at all," she protested. "Trace obviously doesn't think Andy *is* honest or ethical, and certainly not wonderful. But even if he did, he probably wouldn't consider any man good enough for his sister. With your father gone he feels responsible, Bree. Look at it from his point of view."

"Why should I? He never tries to see mine."

"Then be bigger than he is," Hope urged. "If Andy can let it pass, I know you can, too."

After a while, Bree agreed to try. And when she called to say she and Trace had made up enough to speak to each other, Hope felt a glow of satisfaction, knowing she'd had a hand in it.

Therefore she greeted Trace's unexpected appearance in Celebrations a few days later with pleasure instead of trepidation. She'd just come in from a meeting with Erlene's caterer, which hadn't gone well—when did it ever? Sometimes she thought she simply didn't speak "cater-ese."

Trace looked just as good as she remembered, which made her smile even more sincere. "Hi," she greeted him brightly. "What's up?"

"Does something have to be up?" he countered. He glanced around the shop. "Where's your helper?"

"Mrs. Casen? She was here alone most of the day so I sent her home early. Why?"

"I wanted to lure you away for a cup of coffee or a drink, whatever."

"Would you settle for a cup of tea in the back?"

"If I have to." His smile held an edge that told her he wasn't used to settling, period.

He followed her into the office, where she heated the water and made the tea, all the while dying of curiosity to know why he'd come to Celebrations. An electrifying thought occurred to her. Could he be here to ask her out on a date? She'd felt a definite attraction from the very first minute she'd laid eyes on him, at least on her part. Could he have felt it, too? Could it be possible?

Yes!

She put a cup of tea before him and favored him with another brilliant smile. "There you are. Now tell me, what's on your mind?"

"You."

He picked up his cup and looked into its amber depths for a moment, while Hope held her breath. He was going to ask her out. She'd never been so sure of anything in her life.

She realized finally that he was waiting for her to respond, so she did, as innocently as she could. "Me? My goodness, whatever could you want with me?"

He sipped his tea before looking up to trap her in the blue power of his gaze. "I want to..."

Yes, yes! she thought. *You want to ask me out, right*?

"Hire you," he finished his sentence. "Or rather, hire Celebrations to plan an engagement party for our two lovebirds, which is the same thing. How about it, Hope? Want to keep the business in the family?"

Well, that was a bucket of cold water in her face. She stared at him, aghast at what she'd been thinking. Why would a rich, handsome, powerful man like Trace Morgan want to go out with a little nobody working girl like Hope Archer? She'd really let her imagination run away with her this time.

She stalled while trying to pull her wits together. "I don't know, Trace, it might not be a good idea to mix business and—"

"Sure it would." He countered her arguments before she could even finish thinking them up. "It's perfect. Why should I pay strangers when I can pay...well, almost family. We'll practically be brother and sister—"

She recoiled. He grinned. He knew.

"Potential in-laws, at least. So what do you say, Hope? Will you help me out?"

Her resistance melted. He was resigned—no, she preferred to think he was *enthusiastic* about the engagement. Or at least borderline enthusiastic, as indicated by his willingness to give this party. She'd settle for that.

But the fact remained, she wasn't nearly experienced enough to plan the kind of engagement party he would undoubtedly require. "That's terribly nice of you," she began, "but I'm not sure—"

"I am." Putting down his mug, he reached across the small round glass-topped wicker table and took her hands. "Look, it's the least I can do to thank you for putting Sabrina straight."

Her eyes flew wide with alarm. "But I didn't—"

"She told me you did. Hell, she misunderstood what I said at lunch the other day. I was making a bad joke. Andy got it."

"H-he did?"

"Sure. But Bree's so touchy sometimes. I don't know why she has to look for hidden motives in everything I do."

"Gee," Hope whispered, "neither do I." How could anyone suspect hidden motives behind the sincere words and dazzling smile of this absolutely gorgeous male? Sabrina was crazy!

"Look," he coaxed, "all I'm talking about is a little celebration for a few friends. My staff will help you. A nice dinner at the ranch, an announcement and a few toasts to the happy couple. How complicated could it be?"

"Well..." She was weakening. He was right. How complicated could it be?

On the other hand, what did she know about working with anybody's "staff"? She didn't even know if he meant his office staff or his household staff—or even if he *had* a household staff.

Face it, she cautioned herself, you're out of your depth.

"I'm a big tipper," he wheedled.

"Even if I took you up on this, I couldn't take money from you," Hope hedged. "As you pointed out yourself, we're practically family. I couldn't—"

"I wouldn't let you do it, otherwise." His face grew stony. "I wouldn't let you do it for free if you begged me."

She squirmed. "But I wouldn't feel right."

"Hope, the first rule of business is, don't give away what you're selling. I can see I need to take you in hand and teach you a few things . . . about business, of course."

She felt her cheeks warm, but of course, he hadn't meant anything personal. That was all in her mind. "Maybe you should," she conceded. She bit her lip, considering. What if she messed things up? She wouldn't want anyone to think Andy's family was nothing but a bunch of hicks.

On the other hand, she wanted to do it, for a lot of reasons. In her mind's eye, she saw herself in a magnificent gown, airily directing a staff of servants as if to the manor born, then accepting the plaudits of an impressed assemblage of notables.

On the minus side, she didn't even *own* a magnificent gown, and it was more likely he'd expect her to hover in the kitchen with the rest of the hired help.

"Well?" he pressed. He had a curious expression on his face, as if he'd been trying to fathom her thoughts. "You can do it," he said softly, triumphantly, as if he'd just homed in on her wavelength.

"Of course, I can *do* it," she said, trying to convince him he'd misread her, trying to convince herself she could handle this. "If I decide to, that is."

"Okay. I understand." Slowly he lifted her hand to his lips. He hesitated just a kiss away, his breath warm on her fingers when he spoke. "Do it as a personal favor, Hope. Sabrina will be eternally grateful." He kissed her hand. "And so will Andy."

He kissed her hand again, his lips lingering just a tad longer this time. "And so will I."

"I'll do it!" Hope cried, and snatched her burning hand away before he could kiss it again.

How much could one hand take, anyway?

CHAPTER THREE

THROUGH the big front windows of Celebrations, Hope watched Trace drive away. She felt as if she'd been flattened by a steam roller. Mr. Morgan was a powerful individual, in more ways than one. Although he intimidated her, she had agreed to plan the engagement party. She'd given her word, and a promise was a promise.

Even a promise that made her very, *very* nervous.

Sabrina called not a half-hour later. "Trace tells me you're going to do the engagement party," she exclaimed. "Oh, Hope. I can't thank you enough!"

"I'm glad you're pleased," Hope said, meaning it. She mustn't lose sight of the most important thing—the happiness of Andy and Sabrina.

"I'm more than pleased," Sabrina declared. "Can you come to the ranch with Andy Friday night for dinner with Trace and me? Finally the four of us can sit down and do some serious planning."

Serious planning, Hope agreed, was definitely called for. The engagement party would be only the first and easiest of the complications and compromises leading up to the actual ceremony. Even if Bree and Andy tried to stick to their guns about having a simple wedding, something told Hope that might not be possible with Trace in the picture.

Somehow, Hope thought as she hung up the telephone, she must find a way to lead brother and sister to a compromise. Nothing was more important than family. She knew that from bitter experience, having lost so many members of her own. Bree and Trace needed each other. Hope couldn't stand by and let them come to blows over what should be the most joyous occasion of a woman's life—and a happy celebration for her entire family.

Okay, time to get down to business. Hope had a couple of days to bone up on wedding etiquette. Leafing through the Celebrations library of books and magazines, she thought with longing of Aunt Ellen and all her expertise, now lost forever. She'd forgotten more about planning weddings than Hope would ever know.

Still, if Hope worked very hard, and was very, *very* lucky, she should be able to pull off a simple engagement party.

Or so she tried to convince herself.

Andy didn't seem the least bit tense about the evening ahead when he picked Hope up Friday at her small house behind Celebrations. Walking with her cousin to his car, Hope cast him a censorious glance. She felt almost resentful that he didn't share her nervousness.

"You've been to the Flying M before, I take it?" she inquired.

"A couple of times." He held the car door for her, then went around the front to climb in on the driver's side.

"I'm glad you're not as unstrung about this as I am."

He started the engine and pulled away from the curb. "Honey, I'm not marryin' the Flying M. I might have been nervous if I'd known who Bree was before I fell in love with her, but not now. We love each other.'' He gave Hope a broad grin, adding wryly, ''What's to worry?''

What, indeed? Hope sat beside him morosely as they drove away from the Dallas-Fort Worth area. It should take about an hour to get to the ranch gate, Sabrina had said, and she was right.

A sign hung over the private paved road, a Flying M branding iron suspended from a wooden arch with the whole illuminated by floodlights. The gates were closed. Andy slowed the car but before it came to a complete stop, the gates swung majestically open.

''How'd they do that?'' Hope inquired in a whisper.

Andy guided the vehicle forward. ''Closed-circuit TV. Here goes nothing.''

That's the way Hope felt, too.

Andy drove slowly. The night was dark enough that few details were visible except for the towering presence of live oaks bordering white wooden fences on both sides of the road.

They reached a lake, and the road turned to follow the curving shoreline. Topping a slight rise, they started down on the opposite side and saw the house, ablaze with lights, ahead of them.

''Good Lord,'' Hope gasped. ''It looks as big as a hotel!''

And it did, with windows and lawns and gardens and outbuildings illuminated. Hope clasped her icy hands together in her lap.

She couldn't believe she'd thought Trace Morgan was going to ask her for a date! Even in the dark interior of the car, she felt her cheeks burn with embarrassment. Just because she found him fascinating and totally incredible was no reason to lose her grip on reality. She might be loving and giving, but she was no glamour girl and never would be. To a sophisticated man like Trace, she must seem like some little brown mouse.

Andy drove into the parking lot beside the main entryway—a parking lot at a private home! Entirely appropriate, when the home looked more like a country club, Hope thought, reluctantly leaving the security of the car. The front lawn looked as smooth as a putting green, for heaven's sake, even this early in the year.

Taking a deep breath, she glanced at Andy.

Who was beginning to look a tad tense himself. "Into the lion's den," he said gruffly, offering his arm. "What the hell, as Bree said, we can always elope."

"Don't even *think* that." Hope took his arm and a deep breath, following him toward the entry. "Trace went ballistic the last time that word came up. Let's just try to keep everything nice and—"

The door flew open and Sabrina stood there, silhouetted against the brilliant interior. "Andy!" She flung herself into his arms. As if oblivious to everyone and everything else, they kissed.

Hope faded away, feeling like an intruder. How wonderful to be so in love, to be so wrapped up in another person. Misty-eyed, she retreated another step. Sabrina and Andy were just made for each—

She backed into a hard reality. With a muffled cry of apology, she twisted around to find herself practically in Trace's arms. He'd been standing in the doorway, minding his own business, and she'd—

His expression stopped her cold, for he stared at the embracing couple on his doorstep with narrow-eyed distress. *Why, he honestly doubts Andy's feelings*, Hope realized. *Doesn't he recognize true love when he sees it?*

Perhaps not, but he certainly recognized Hope's anxiety. When he glanced at her and saw her expression, his own changed, transformed in an instant to a pleasant smile of greeting. Little tingles traveled all the way down to her toes.

"Welcome to the Flying M," he said. Stepping aside, he gestured to the open doorway. "Please come in."

"T-thank you." Had she imagined that troubled look on his face? Pondering, Hope walked into the dramatic two-story entryway and stopped short. She was surrounded by glass and crystal and gleaming wood, and the very opulence stunned her.

A laughing Sabrina brushed past, dragging Andy with her. "Hi, Hope," she exclaimed. "I'm so glad you're here. Come on—we'll have a drink before dinner."

Still awed by her surroundings, Hope surrendered her coat to a maid who'd appeared silently, then turned to Trace for guidance. He took her arm and steered her after the other couple, through a series of huge, high-ceilinged rooms, finally coming to a halt in what must be as close as this house was likely to get to cozy.

A fire snapped and crackled and leaped in a marble fireplace. The room itself, spacious and airy, was all white carpet and white furniture, pale polished woods and soaring columns. It looked like something out of a decorating magazine, not a place where real people lived.

Sabrina walked behind a curving bar fronted by four stools. "We need to start this auspicious evening with a toast," she declared happily. Pulling out four champagne flutes, she indicated the bottle of wine cooling on the countertop in a crystal bucket.

Trace started forward but Sabrina didn't seem to notice. With eyes only for Andy, she added, "Will you do the honors, darling? And don't spill a drop! Bad luck for engagement toasts, you know."

Trace's expression turned bleak, then grew hard and determined. Hope took a step toward him and said quickly, "Your home is beautiful." She touched his arm lightly to distract him. "I don't believe I've ever been in such a magnificent house."

"I'm glad you like it." He spoke absently, but then he drew in a light breath and turned that megawatt smile directly upon her. "Sometimes it's like living in a mausoleum but I suppose a person can get used to anything, given enough time."

Hope laughed lightly. "That's what they say." She led the way toward the tall leather-cushioned bar stools and slid onto one, inviting him to join her with a gesture.

The cork shot out of the bottle in Andy's hands, and Sabrina gave a delighted squeal. Hope held her breath while sparkling wine bubbled high above the bottle's mouth. Not that she was superstitious or anything. But not a drop spilled over, and she laughed with approval.

"A match made in heaven!" she declared, watching Andy pour champagne into the elegant crystal flutes held ready by Sabrina. She accepted her wine and waited until all held their glasses. "So who will have the honor of the first toast?"

Sabrina glanced around the small circle, her happy expression turning a bit wary. "Trace," she decreed. "The brother of the bride gets first crack at the happy couple."

"Sabrina!" Hope glanced anxiously at the tall man at her side.

But Trace was all charm and grace as he lifted his wine. "To my favorite sister," he intoned with appropriate solemnity. "May she always be as happy as she is at this moment."

Hope started to drink, then realized Sabrina hadn't and halted in confusion. Bree stared at her brother, a clear challenge in her blue eyes. Her hand tightened on Andy's arm, stopping him when he would have lifted his wineglass to his lips.

Trace dipped his chin in brief acknowledgment to her unspoken demand. "And to Andrew Archer, the man she's chosen. Cheers."

Still Bree's icy blue gaze held steady on her brother.

What else does she expect of him? Hope wondered. Without hesitation, she threw herself into the breach. "Congratulations to a wonderful couple. May your marriage give new meaning to that wonderful old cliché, happily ever after."

Deliberately, she drank.

So did the others. Andy looked a little confused but not concerned. Trace shot Hope one glance that might have been grateful, and Sabrina chose to accept Hope's compromise in the spirit in which it had been offered.

"So," Sabrina said, placing her flute on the bar, "when shall we announce our engagement? How about next Saturday?"

Trace shook his head. "Too soon. That wouldn't give Hope time to do her thing. How about four weeks from tonight?"

"Too long!" Sabrina gave him an incensed glance.

"Three weeks from tonight?" Trace bargained.

"Can't," Andy said. "I've got a business trip coming up. I'll be out of town."

"Five weeks, then." Trace sounded pleased. "Now that's settled—"

"Not a chance." Bree, already on the defensive, was angry again. "Two weeks. Right, Andy? And not a day later or we'll just skip a formal announcement and go ahead and get married."

Trace looked alarmed but quickly smoothed over his sudden tension. "Now, don't be hasty." He turned to Hope as if seeking her support. "Can you get things ready that quickly? I wouldn't want to cause you any trouble."

Hope felt trapped between brother and sister. "That's what I do," she reminded him. "Certainly we can be ready in two weeks—depending, of course, on what kind of party you'd like."

"Formal sit-down dinner," Trace said promptly.

"Cocktail party," Sabrina said just as quickly. "An announcement, a few toasts—"

Andy rolled his eyes. "Wham, bam, thank you, ma'am—is that what you've got in mind?" he asked Sabrina.

"Whose side are you on?" She looked crest-fallen, and perhaps a bit betrayed.

"Yours, sweetheart, just as soon as I figure out what you really want, as opposed to what you *say* you want just to irritate your brother."

Oh, Lord, Hope thought, this is *not* going to be easy! "Why don't we talk about the guest list first, and then decide what would be appropriate based on that?" she broke in. "How many will you be inviting?"

"About fifty," Trace declared.

"A dozen or so." Sabrina leaned over the bar until her stubborn face was only a few inches from her brother's. "Trace, what are you trying to pull here?"

"Not a damn thing. I just don't want to hurt anybody's feelings by leaving them out." He leaned back on his bar stool, all innocent bewilderment. "Furthermore, the more people we invite to the party, the more money Celebrations will make. But if you don't care about—"

"You know I care but—"

"Both of you, stop!" Hope looked from brother to sister, wishing she could make them see how ridiculous they were behaving. They were turning a delightful occasion into a duel. "We have only one thing to consider here—well, maybe two."

Trace cocked his head and smiled at her as if she were his ally. "And that is?"

"First of all, we must consider the bride and groom."

Sabrina stuck out her tongue in triumph. "See?" she taunted Trace. "This is *my* wedding and what I say goes!"

"Sabrina, I'm shocked at you."

Sabrina frowned. "But Hope, I thought... You just said..."

Hope softened any implied criticism by patting Sabrina's hand. "It's *your* marriage, but the wedding and all the wonderful events leading up to it are for those who love you, as much as they are for you and Andy. Don't get so wrapped up in sibling rivalry that you end up slighting those who will want to share your happiness."

Sabrina hung her head. "Oh, all right. I didn't mean to sound selfish—a tendency I find myself constantly fighting." She looked up with that charming Morgan smile. "So what do you recommend, Ms. Party Planner?"

"I recommend we hear from Andy, who hasn't said a word."

"Good idea," agreed the bride-to-be.

All three turned to the bridegroom-to-be. He proved equal to the occasion.

"How about this," he proposed. "A good ol' Texas barbecue two weeks from today—that'll be March twenty-fifth—served buffet style with as many people as any of us feel like inviting. Can you pull that off, Hope?"

"Sure, but—" She glanced anxiously at Trace. "Does that work for you? If you'll give up formality for numbers—"

"Then I'll give up numbers for informality," Sabrina interjected. "What do you say, Trace? Is it a bargain?"

A slow, ironic smile curved his lips, a smile that touched his blue eyes when he looked from his sister to Hope. "It's a bargain," he agreed. "Let's drink to it."

They did, raising their glasses with an enthusiasm that had been lacking earlier. Only later, on their way into the dining room, did Trace take Hope's arm and whisper in her ear.

"Quite the little peacemaker, aren't you?"

"I'm sorry if I overstepped my bounds."

He slid one arm around her waist and gave her a quick squeeze that almost dropped her in her tracks with trembling reaction.

"Not at all. What I really wanted to say was thank you. You've averted the first crisis. If you can just keep it up, you'll be worth your weight in gold—and so will Celebrations."

All through an elegant dinner, she worried that he might have thought she'd been guiding them with professional aplomb. Little did he know!

She'd been guiding them with her heart, nothing more.

They took dessert and coffee in an upstairs billiards room, where Sabrina promptly challenged Andy to a game and proceeded, in her words, to "beat the pants off him." Hope and Trace settled on a comfortable overstuffed sofa and watched the mock-fierce contest while nibbling on extravagant seven-layer hazelnut torte.

It was becoming crystal clear to Hope that Trace needed her "expertise" to plan a simple engagement party like he needed a rent-controlled apartment. She sighed. If she wasn't careful, she was likely to make a spectacle of herself, both personally and professionally.

"Something wrong?" Trace placed his crystal dessert plate and silver fork on an end table, then picked up his coffee cup and saucer.

She shook her head quickly. Mashing cake crumbs on the tines of her fork, she searched for a neutral subject. And settled upon the obvious.

"You must have a wonderful cook," she ventured. "Dinner was superb, and this torte is to die for."

Trace smiled easily. "Ingrid will be delighted to hear you think so."

"Ingrid is your cook?"

"Yes. She's only been with us for a few years but we're quite satisfied. She'll be at your disposal when you plan the party, of course, as will Lillian, the housekeeper. Lillian's been with the family for more than thirty years, so she pretty much knows everybody's likes and dislikes. She should be a big help to you."

Hope felt her stomach clench. The ranch housekeeper had already been employed by the Morgans for five years before Hope was even born! She'd probably just love taking orders—or even suggestions—from a little upstart outsider.

Trace continued. "Of course, it takes more than those two to keep this place running, but we'll hire outside help as needed."

"I ... see."

"Do you?" He arched one dark brow, looking at her with amusement.

"I think I do," she said slowly, holding her dessert plate on her lap in a nervous grip. "To tell you the truth, Trace, I'm a little overwhelmed. At first I thought you hired Celebrations just to be nice."

"You did, did you?" With elegant long fingers, he lifted his cup to well-shaped lips and drank. "And now what do you think?"

"Now I think you hired me to keep peace," she said candidly. "You knew it would please Sabrina, and perhaps take her mind off your lack of enthusiasm for this wedding."

He inclined his dark head in what might have been acknowledgment. "If I thought that having you around would distract Sabrina, I seem to have been mistaken," he said. "She's already been on my case half a dozen times tonight."

"Yes," Hope admitted. "But you did seem pleasantly surprised earlier with my penchant for compromise—in fact, I have a sneaking suspicion you were counting on it. However," she added primly, "I don't want you to think that's what I agreed to do. You engaged me to plan a party, and I will—a barbecue buffet two weeks from tonight for fifty—" she rolled her eyes "—for fifty guests. That shouldn't be too difficult."

"Unless Barbecue Bob is already booked."

"Barbecue *who?*"

"Bob. Barbecue Bob makes the greatest Texas barbecue in—" He gestured expansively. "In the entire state of Texas, which is the same as saying in the world. Promise him anything. Tell him he can come out here, dig pits, put up smokehouses, the sky's the limit. But we've got to have Barbecue Bob's barbecue or—"

"Don't say it! We're not rescheduling!"

"Quick, aren't you?" He grinned. "Just remember, I wanted a sit-down dinner. You can serve *anything* at a sit-down dinner."

She could see nothing malicious behind his teasing. In fact, his beautiful blue eyes gleamed with good humor. Her cheeks grew warm as she looked at him, silently acknowledging that he was at once the most attractive, charming, *manipulative* man she'd ever met. Which also made him the most dangerous—to her, but also to her cousin and the woman he loved.

"I wish you knew Andy better," Hope burst out. "If you did, you'd realize there's no need to worry about this marriage and you'd stop trying to throw up roadblocks."

"Whoa, hold your horses." He spoke lazily but with an increasingly familiar steel underpinning. "It's not a marriage. It's not even an engagement until the formal announcement is made in two weeks. Even then, nothing's carved in granite. They can always change their minds right up to the moment they say 'I do.'"

"Well, sure. But my point is that Andy's such a wonderful guy, once you get to know him you'll be thrilled to have him in your family."

"Perhaps," he conceded indifferently. He held her gaze. "Did it ever occur to you that my reservations might have as much to do with my sister as with your cousin?"

"No, of course not." Her eyes flew wide. "Sabrina's a wonderful girl, and obviously very close to you except for this one problem."

"Rather an important one, wouldn't you say?"

"Yes, but not insurmountable. Are you saying you'd feel exactly the same no matter who she wanted to marry?"

"Yes . . . and no."

He put down his cup and saucer, then placed her empty dessert plate on the table. He took her hands in his and looked deep into her eyes. She reeled beneath the impact, her fingers tightening on his in reaction. Did this man know his own power to disturb? Surely not . . .

"Hope," he said earnestly, "my reservations are not exactly coming out of left field. There are reasons I—"

"What on earth are you two whispering about?"

Sabrina's voice jarred Hope out of a near trance. She yanked her hands from Trace's and jumped to her feet. "Nothing. I mean, we were just talking about the food—for the engagement dinner, I mean. We—"

"Hey," Andy said, "we're not accusing you of plotting or anything. Sit down, be cool. We've got something to say to both of you."

Hope sat down abruptly, her heart skipping a beat in her befuddlement. A glance at Trace showed her that he, too, was bracing for the coming announcement.

Bree snuggled in Andy's arms, looking flushed and pretty. "Relax," she advised. "It's something good." She turned her smile on Hope. "I'd like you to be my maid of honor," she said all in a rush. "I want to be part of your family and have you be part of mine. I already know you well enough to like you a lot but we'll become even closer if you'll do this for me. Will you? Please, say yes!"

"I—I..." Emotional tears leaped into Hope's eyes. "Oh, Sabrina, I'm so honored, but wouldn't you rather invite a girlfriend, someone you grew up with, a relative? It's not as if I was Andy's sister. I'm only his cousin—"

"But he loves you like a sister, and so do I," Sabrina insisted. "Please, Hope? There's no one I'd rather have. Say you'll do it."

Hope looked from Bree's shining face to Andy's equally encouraging expression. "D-do *you* want me to do this?" she asked him softly.

"Yeah," he said. "Yeah, Hope, I do." He shuffled his feet, looking embarrassed. "You *are* like a sister to me. But it was her idea, honest."

Laughing, crying with pleasure, Hope threw her arms around the happy couple. "In that case, I'm honored," she choked out. With a final squeeze, she stepped back, brushing tears from her cheeks. "My goodness," she declared, "that was quite a surprise."

Andy's gaze narrowed slightly. "Think so? Then how about this for a topper?" Squaring his shoulders, he faced Trace, who'd watched everything with a faint, suspicious expression on his lean face. "Trace, Bree tells me her Grandfather Morgan will be coming from Florida to give her away."

"That's right, if his health allows. So?"

"So I'd like you to be my best man for all the reasons Bree said—so we can all be one big happy family and so forth and so on."

Andy thrust out his jaw as if he expected his future brother-in-law to take a swing at it. "So what do you say to that?"

"I say..." Trace stood up slowly, his eyes turbulent. He shook his head as if he couldn't believe what he'd heard. "I say you've got a hell of a lot of nerve, Archer!"

"You caught him by surprise," Hope argued as she and Andy drove away from the mansion commonly and mistakenly referred to as a ranch house. "He calmed right down, didn't he?"

"Big deal. What about you? Didn't Sabrina catch *you* by surprise? You didn't blow up like a stick of dynamite."

"He apologized. He even said he'd think it over. Give him a break, will you, Andy?"

"Yeah, he apologized—to keep Bree from packing her bags. And if I'm not mistaken, the apology was more to you, for subjecting you to a scene, than to the rest of us."

"Andy..."

"What?"

Hope chewed on her bottom lip for a moment, thinking carefully about what she was going to say. "I don't think Trace really has much of anything against you."

"Huh?" In the faint light of the dashboard, he gave her a skeptical glance. "You're losin' your marbles, babe. What makes you say that?"

"Just a hunch. I think he's got his doubts about Sabrina. He was about to explain when the two of you dropped your bombshell."

"Yeah?" Andy didn't sound convinced.

"Maybe he's just overprotective, or maybe he just doubts her judgment or maybe—" She bit off her musings, unwilling to say anything that might lead Andy to think she was disloyal to him or to his fiancée. But the fact was, she'd had the strongest impression that Trace was about to tell her Sabrina had made mistakes with men in the past.

"Maybe what?" Andy pressed.

"Maybe nothing. I suppose he thinks the life you're offering Sabrina is so different from the one she's used to that she won't be able to handle the changes . . . that she's too spoiled to adapt—"

"Aw, hell." Andy's tone was cynical. "He thinks I'm a damned fortune hunter. That's what he *really* thinks."

"Of course!" Hope sank back on the car seat. Why hadn't she thought of that? Andy was right. With the kind of money the Morgans had, they must be primed for fortune hunters. How awful for them, especially when they were both so attractive and bright and successful and charming and—

Andy laughed, and once again became the cousin she loved. "Only you, Hope," he said affectionately. "Only you would need to have something that simple pointed out to you."

"Don't pick on me." She gave him an equally affectionate punch on the arm. "But if that's the problem, all you have to do is sign a prenuptial agreement. Then Trace will know you're not some fortune hunter and—"

"No dice. I suggested that to Sabrina at the very beginning but she's got her dander up about this and won't budge. She says what's mine is hers and what's hers is mine. And you know what? I don't give a hoot in hell about her money but I can see her point."

Hope could, too. Sharing was a big part of the commitment of marriage, sharing everything, the good along with the bad.

Who would ever have thought a great fortune could be part of the bad?

CHAPTER FOUR

ON MONDAY, Trace himself introduced Hope to the Flying M housekeeper, sweeping aside Sabrina's offer to do the honors. Hope found Lillian to be more than a little reserved, which was no great surprise.

She's going to make me prove myself, Hope thought as they chatted about the engagement party. *Well, I don't blame her one little bit. She doesn't know me from Adam.*

When a telephone call took Trace to his office on the first floor, Lillian led Hope through the rest of the magnificent mansion. She'd been impressed Saturday, but what she saw now really made her nervous. This house was big even for Texas!

Everything was not only spacious and elegant but somehow more comfortable than seemed possible in such grand surroundings. Fireplaces abounded— a total of six throughout the house, Lillian said— and fresh flowers were everywhere. When the housekeeper led the way into what she called "the great room," Hope gasped with delight. Two-story windows overlooked both a private lake and an enormous swimming pool complete with hundred-foot lap lanes.

"We can seat fifty or sixty in here comfortably for a meal," Lillian said. "The bar is normally set up against that wall and if you want buffet tables—'' She hesitated, her eyes narrowing as she looked at Hope. "Is there a problem?"

Hope gave a weak laugh, putting out a hand to touch the back of a cushioned chair. "This... this..." Her gesture was all-inclusive. "All this just takes my breath away."

The guarded expression in Lillian's gray eyes seemed to soften before Hope's candor. "Honey," she drawled, "it's just a house. Don't let it intimidate you. Trace and Sabrina, unlike a few Morgans I could name, are real folks despite all this."

"How could they be?" Hope spread her hands helplessly and looked to Lillian for answers. "The rich really *are* different, aren't they? I can't imagine how Andy's going to fit in."

"I wouldn't worry about that...much. Andy seems like a young man who knows what he wants and where to find it. To tell you the truth—" Lillian laughed, much less starchy now than she'd been before "—I don't imagine you could melt Andy and pour him in this house for more than a few hours at a stretch."

"You're right about that," Hope agreed.

"Sabrina, now..." Lillian shook her silvery head doubtfully. "This is all she's ever known so it's a wonder she turned out as good as she did. It won't hurt her to see how the other half lives, though, I can tell you that."

"Maybe so," Hope said, more to be polite than because she had any particular opinion on the subject. "I don't know which would be harder, growing up with all this and leaving it behind, or growing up normal and then being plunked down in the middle of such opulence." She shuddered. "Better Andy and Sabrina than me," she added with heartfelt sincerity.

"You'd be surprised how quick you could get used to all this," Lillian predicted, "if you approached it with an open mind—and you strike me as a young woman with a very open mind. Let's go on out to the kitchen and meet the cook. Then it's time for some serious talk about this big hoop-de-do comin' up."

Ingrid, the cook, a good thirty years younger than the sixty-something housekeeper, was instantly welcoming. She did, however, seem a bit annoyed when informed that Barbecue Bob would be catering most of the food. Still, she took it philosophically.

"In that case, I'll make up a bunch of those peach pies the bossman is so crazy about," she offered, quickly adding, "that is, if it's all right with you, Ms. Archer. Trace said we were to—" She glanced at Lillian and clamped her mouth shut.

"Trace told you what?" Hope asked quickly. Darn it, if he was going to pay Celebrations to plan a party, he should let her earn her money!

"Nothing," Lillian soothed. "All he told us was to cooperate with you—and that what you say goes! So if you don't think peach pies will do it . . ."

"It'll be perfect," Hope said firmly. "Ingrid, if your peach pie is even half as good as that cake I ate here Saturday night, it'll steal ol' Barbecue Bob's thunder right out from under him!"

"Why, thanks," Ingrid said, accepting such effusive praise as her due. "Speaking of which, I'm just about to take a few loaves of bread out of the

tender says he'll need more space and the photographer—"

"Everything will be fine."

Puzzled by his total assurance, she cocked her head and met his gaze, finally bursting out, "How can you be so sure?"

"Because," he said, "I wouldn't have it any other way."

'Oh." That stopped her cold. "Do you always get your way?"

"Always." His bland smile did not conceal his intensity.

Poor Andy! "Uh..." She tried to think of a polite way to say what needed saying. "Are you feeling... better about the engagement?"

For a long time, he didn't reply. Then he shrugged. "Perhaps...some better. You know, Hope, if they really love each other..."

"Not *if*!" His hardheaded refusal to acknowledge the obvious was a constant frustration to her.

"If they're really in love," he continued, completely unflappable, "nothing anyone else can say or do will make the least bit of difference."

"That's not true," she objected. "Disapproval hurts, especially when it comes from family."

"Not in the long run. If Sabrina and Andy marry and live happily ever after, all the doubters will come around. But if they marry for the wrong reasons..."

She frowned. "What kind of reasons?"

"Oh, I don't know." He looked at her in feigned innocence but with sharp meaning behind his blue eyes. "Just for the sake of argument, if either of them wanted to marry to prove a point to someone else...or for money...or for shock value...or even on a whim..."

Hope put the remaining half of her sandwich on the plate. She longed to tell him he was wrong, that none of those reasons applied to either Andy or Sabrina. But there was something about his expression that stopped her. It was almost as if he were talking about someone else, or even from bitter experience.

So all she said was, "I'm truly sorry you still have reservations, Trace. I can see you're one of the doubters who'll eventually have to come around."

The smile that touched his well-shaped lips was almost sad. "They're not married yet," he reminded her. "If and when they are—well, I'll sure as hell be rooting for them."

Hope shivered. Surely Trace would become resigned to this marriage, if not enthusiastic. Surely he—

His hand settled possessively on her shoulder and blasted away all rational thought. She jerked her head around to stare at him, lips parting in a question.

"You shivered," he said, rubbing the curve of her shoulder down to her upper arm. "Are you cold?"

"N-no—yes, but—" She swallowed hard, trying to ignore the shivers of pleasure that radiated through her body from the point where his hand rested. "I'll warm up as soon as I get back to work, which I've got to do right now."

She dipped her shoulder to dislodge his hand, then stood up. "Thanks for lunch," she said brightly. "I'll see you tonight at the party." She took a step, then stopped. "Cross your fingers," she pleaded.

"For you? Glad to." He made a great show of doing so.

"For all of us," she corrected, but she wasn't sure he heard her, for she was already turning away.

Hours later, Hope sneaked into the kitchen for the dozenth time since the party began, to catch her breath and make sure everything was running smoothly. Sidestepping one of Barbecue Bob's servers carrying an enormous slab of beef on its way to the buffet table, she nearly bumped into Lillian.

Lillian gave a thumbs-up. "Lookin' good out there," she said, her expression pleased. "You must be tickled pink, especially now that the band's arrived."

Hope was tickled pink, all right, but not about the band. The engagement announcement was a hurdle cleanly and brilliantly handled by Trace. Hope and Andy were officially engaged. What could possibly go wrong now?

Slipping into the great room, Hope took in the scene with a measuring glance. The guests seemed to be enjoying themselves, milling around between the buffet tables and the bar. The majority wore Western clothing in deference to the invitations so painstakingly lettered by Hope herself. They'd greeted the engagement announcement with enthusiasm although the majority had never met Andy or had the slightest idea who he might be.

"Who's that?"

Trace's voice, right in her ear, stirring the curling tendrils of hair escaping from the gingham headband she'd tied around her brown hair. She shivered and resisted the urge to turn toward him. "W-who?" she asked.

"That guy over there talking to Andy."

"Oh, that guy." Hope wasn't pleased. "That's George Archer."

"Ah, a relative of yours?" His tone was amused.

She sighed. "Afraid so. An uncle, actually. Don't tell me he got hold of you."

"Yes, but I managed to make my getaway. Care to dance?"

Before she could think of a reason not to, he whirled her into his arms and laughed into her shocked face. "Wonderful party," he complimented her.

"Thanks." She tried to pull away without making a scene but he held her much too closely. "Trace!" She braced her palms on his chest. "I—I feel a little awkward dancing when I'm supposed to be working. I mean, I know I'm here as Andy's cousin, too, but—"

"Nope, you're here as my guest," he said smoothly. "Why do you think I don't have a date?"

"W-why—" She bit her lip. She'd wondered about that, dreading the thought of seeing him with some sleek and beautiful debutante—and overjoyed when it hadn't happened.

"I'll tell you why," he said, his tone teasing. "Because I wanted to be free to devote all my attention to the happy couple... and to you."

"Me?" She stared up at him, wide-eyed.

"That's right, you. I feel a certain responsibility for dragging you into this. Besides, we've got a lot to celebrate, wouldn't you agree?"

She softened. "Does that mean you're reconciled to—"

Across his shoulder, she saw Bree and Andy in unexpectedly intense conversation. Suddenly Bree whirled and ran out of the room through a side door.

"What is it?" Trace twisted to look over his shoulder, in so doing pulling Hope even more snugly against him.

"I'm not sure." Something warned her not to tell him what she'd seen. He was so protective toward his sister that he'd doubtless blame Andy for her unhappiness whether it was his fault or not. She added as a smoke screen, "Can I take a rain check on the dance? I need to find someone to pick up all those dirty glasses on that table over there."

"Forget the glasses." He whirled her a few steps. He was a wonderful dancer—naturally.

"Your great-aunt is scaring that waitress to death over by the door, shouting at her. I should go to the rescue."

"The old lady's deaf. She shouts at everybody." His smile coaxed Hope to do things she knew she shouldn't.

"And isn't that one of your business associates, waving from the doorway?"

He danced her in a circle so he could see, then swore under his breath. "Yeah, that's one of 'em, all right. If I let you go, will you promise—"

"I promise," she agreed breathlessly. Sliding her hands to his elbows, she pushed out of his arms.

"I'll hold you to that," he said in a low voice meant for her ears alone.

She hoped he would.

At least, she hoped he would, until she found Sabrina weeping in Andy's arms in the barren winter garden. "What is it?" she exclaimed, teeth already chattering from the chill night air—and perhaps dread. "What's happened?"

Bree clung tighter to Andy, her fists clenching in his cowboy shirt. "I hate him!" she wailed. "I know he doesn't approve—he'll never approve— but he's not going to get away with this!"

"Now, honey." Andy stroked her back, while giving Hope a look of entreaty. "You're jumping to conclusions. We don't know that Trace is behind this."

"He's behind it, all right." She leaned back in his arms, her face tear-streaked and angry. "I'll never forgive him, never!"

Hope looked anxiously at her cousin for coherent answers. "Andy?"

He sighed. "It's not as bad as she's letting on. I got a job offer yesterday."

"So?"

"So it's the job of my dreams, the kind of job any environmental engineer would kill for."

Sabrina sobbed louder.

Hope said again, "So?"

"So the job is in California."

"California!" Bree repeated the word, ending it on a wail of disbelief. "I see my brother's fine hand in this. This is his not-too-subtle way of trying to separate us. Well, he's not going to get away with it!''

Hope touched Bree's shoulder anxiously. "Wait a minute, wait a minute. Why don't we all sit down and consider this logically?'' She indicated a grouping of wrought-iron garden furniture, hoping her expression didn't betray how sick she felt at the possibility that Trace really was plotting against them.

"What's to consider?'' Instead of sitting, Bree began to pace, her misery quickly making way for rising fury.

Andy watched Bree, his expression haunted. "In the first place,'' he said, "we don't know Trace is behind this. Maybe I got this offer because—well, hell, maybe because I'm good at what I do.''

Bree stopped short. "Of course you are, darling. But how would anyone in California know that? He did it. He did it and he'll pay!''

"Okay, for the sake of argument, let's assume your brother *is* behind it. So what?''

"So what!'' Bree and Hope responded in unison, staring at Andy as if he'd just committed treason.

Andy shrugged. "Hey, I didn't just fall off the banana boat. I considered the possibility that Trace was behind the job offer before I even mentioned it to you, Bree. I knew how you'd react.''

Hope glanced from one to the other. "Then why on earth are the two of you letting this upset you so?''

"Because—dammit, a job like this doesn't come along every day. It's perfect for me. I can do this job better than anybody in the country, and I want the chance to prove it.''

"But Andy!" Once again, tears streaked Bree's cheeks.

He moved to her quickly and took her in his arms. "I want to succeed for both our sakes, honey. Can't you understand that? Why shouldn't I take the job? If it works out, you can join me there after the wedding. If it doesn't, I know I can find something here again."

She clung to him with an intensity that made Hope's vision blur with tears and her lips tremble.

"Bree, our love is strong enough to survive a few weeks apart." Andy kissed her hair. "Besides, planes fly both ways."

Bree lifted her face. "They do, don't they?" she whispered. "It's just that— You know I love you, Andy. If this job means so much to you—"

He kissed away her tears and then his lips touched hers. Openly weeping, Hope stumbled down the garden path, humbled by the depth of the love Bree and Andy held for each other. Thank heaven she hadn't let Trace shake her faith in them! Thank heaven—

She stopped outside the door, shivering violently but loath to go inside just yet. Trace *had* shaken her faith, whether she wanted to admit it or not. Like Bree, Hope had doubted the depth of Andy's feelings when he declared his eagerness to tackle the new job. Also like Bree, Hope was now filled with guilt at her lack of faith.

Trace wanted to break them up, no two ways about it. Like a fool, Hope had thought him above such machinations. Why, she'd actually defended him!

Opening the door, she marched inside. The first person she saw was Trace, talking to—oh, no, not Uncle George, as close to a black sheep as the Archer family had. But they'd seen her. She had no choice but to join them.

George downed the last of his beer and grinned. "Was just tellin' Trace here, nice to see the Archers movin' up in the world," the paunchy man boomed. "Ol' Andy's got himself a real sweet little setup here."

"What?" Aghast, Hope stared at her uncle. "Are you drunk, George? I hope so, to say a thing like that."

"Now, don't get your dander up." George held up his hands in a defensive gesture. "I was just talkin' to my good buddy, Trace, here, about a job. No need to get in an uproar or nothin'."

He backed away into the crowd. Completely humiliated, she turned to Trace, but before she could say anything, he swept her into his arms. He looked, for all the world, like the cat that swallowed the cream. "You promised me a dance," he reminded her, his tone silky and caressing.

"No, thank you." The ice in her throat frosted her words.

He recoiled. "What the hell?"

"Not here." She glanced around at the people surrounding them. "When the party's over—"

"No. Now."

Grabbing her hand, he half-led, half-dragged her through the door, down the wide hallway and up the stairs. He seemed oblivious to the stares of those they passed, but she wasn't. Her cheeks burned with humiliation but all she could do was lift her chin and try to appear unconcerned.

He hauled her into the billiards room and shut the door. Turning to face her, he looked straight into her eyes.

"Okay," he said in a no-nonsense tone, "what's going on?"

Hope whirled, her denim skirt swirling around her legs. Thrusting her hands into the pockets, she walked a few steps away from him.

"I'm waiting," came that implacable voice from behind her.

Taking a deep breath for courage, she faced him again. Why did he have to look so good? she wondered miserably. Sportswear, business suits, jeans—the man looked great in anything. Even that unyielding expression failed to dim his appeal.

"Sabrina's very upset," she blurted.

"Is she? Why? Somebody insult her engagement ring?"

"Oh! Do you really think she's that shallow?" Hope clenched her fists in impotent fury. All the times she should have confronted this man but failed to do so seemed to crowd in on her, making this moment even worse because she'd resisted it so long and so hard.

"Sabrina's not shallow. Spoiled, perhaps, but not shallow." He strolled to the bulky billiards table and leaned negligently on one corner, crossing his booted feet at the ankle. "If that's not it—" He waited, as a jaguar waits for its prey to make a mistake.

"Andy's been offered another job, a job he's really eager to take."

"Good for him. So what's the problem?"

So cool. So unmoved. She gritted her teeth. "It's in California."

"Fancy that." He glanced around. "Would you like a drink? Should be something in the refrigerator under the wet bar."

"No, I don't want anything to drink! I want straight answers, but I don't suppose I'll get them from you."

She tried to sweep past him with regal hauteur, but he stepped into her path and caught her by the upper arms. Hot anger suddenly swirled just beneath his carefully controlled surface.

"Ask me anything you like," he challenged. "I've never lied to you. You have no reason to accuse me of dishonesty, Hope Archer."

She met his hard gaze but it wasn't easy. "Sabrina thinks you arranged for Andy to be offered that job just to separate them," she said, unnerved by the tremor she heard in her voice. She swallowed hard and closed her eyes. "Did you? Did you do it, Trace?" And then in spite of herself, she opened her eyes and stared into his. "Tell me you didn't and I'll believe you," she cried.

CHAPTER FIVE

TRACE didn't flinch before the accusation in Hope's eyes. He seemed completely unaffected by her demeanor. In fact, when he spoke, his manner couldn't have been more offhand. "I mentioned Andy to a friend who owns an environmental consulting firm, which happens to be in California. Had Andy not been qualified, no amount of pressure on my part would have got him the offer. So... yeah, you can give me the credit, if you want to."

"Credit!" She tried to shake off his hold on her, without success. "That was a low-down, underhanded, miserable—"

"Whoa!"

She considered his indignant expression to be as phony as everything else about this conversation. He wasn't in the least bit ashamed of what he'd done, that much was obvious.

"So the kitten has claws. She isn't always loving and giving," he drawled. "Before you rip me apart with them, tell me—how does Andy feel about this?"

"Ask him. We're talking about Sabrina." She added hastily, just in case he thought she had any sympathy for him, "And me, too, of course. I think it was an awful thing for you to do."

"Why 'of course'?"

"Because you're obviously trying to come between them," she declared, sorry she sounded so blustery but needing to impress him with the seriousness of his offense. She didn't often get this upset, and his utter control made her even more uncomfortable with her own loss of same.

"I don't see how putting Andy in line for a better job falls into the category of—"

"Don't play games with me, Trace! Sabrina can't go to California with him, not until school's out for the summer, anyway. Andy takes his responsibilities very seriously, and that includes responsibility for supporting a wife. All he can see is a chance for advancement, but if he takes it they'll be separated for months!"

His glance was reproachful, as if she'd somehow let him down. "Hope, if they love each other, it won't make any difference."

"Of course they love each other, but—" She floundered. She hated arguing with anyone, but especially with him. He seemed to sense her weak spots and go straight for them. He was also trying to overwhelm her with logic—never her strong suit. She was the type who depended more on feelings.

Her feelings at the moment warned her to run for her life and take Bree and Andy with her. If she didn't, Trace might very well convince her that up was really down, that north was really south.

So she turned away. It would be easier to defy him when she didn't have to look at the sexy cleft in his chin or the triumphant gleam in his long-lashed blue eyes.

"Don't you think true love can survive such tests?" He rested his hands on her shoulders and added more sharply, "Turn around and look at me. I don't like talking to your back.'

"I—I don't want to look at you, or talk to you, either. I'm going back to the party."

"No, you're not. You're going to face me."

She had no choice, she told herself as he turned her slowly around. But even as she rationalized her weakness, she reveled in the intimacy of his voice, his expression, his nearness.

He was her weakness. She had never known anyone like Trace Morgan. Perhaps there *was* no one like him.

"That's better." He slid one hand up to curve around her throat in a tentative caress. "Listen, Hope. I've done them a favor. They can't lose. If Andy takes the job and Bree can't handle it, they weren't meant to be together. If he turns down the job to make her happy, then…well, that will prove something, too."

"But—"

"If you've got so much faith in them, let them handle this on their own."

"Trace!" She brought her fists down on his chest in a light blow of frustration. "Will you let me get a word in edgewise?"

"No," he said around a smile that was almost a grimace, and kissed her.

Hope could not have been more surprised if he had slapped her. Although she knew he was only kissing her to shut her up, she found she couldn't pass up this opportunity to savor something she'd thought so much about—dreamed about, in her weaker moments.

Trace was out of her league and she knew it—not because of his wealth but because of his powerful personality. This was the first time she'd ever dredged up the strength to defy him and here he was, making mincemeat of her objections.

And even worse, making her like it. Shocked though she was to immobility, still she fell helplessly under the spell of his kiss. Which, of course, was as outstanding as everything else about him. Was there nothing this man couldn't do? Was there no way she could defend herself from him?

He lifted his head and looked at her with a kind of dark perplexity. "I'm glad you're willing to listen to reason," he said ironically, his mouth quirking down at one corner.

"Reason? I don't think so." Dizzy with unfamiliar feelings, she braced her hands against his chest. Her head began to clear and she drew away from him, gaining strength with distance. "I *do* have faith in Bree and Andy but I'm not going to let you—"

The sound of an opening door interrupted her impassioned speech, and she heard Bree say with barely controlled anger, "Andy and I have something we want to say to you, Trace."

Trace's expression didn't change, except for the very faintest tightening, which wouldn't have been visible had Hope not been standing so near and watching him so closely.

"Shall I go?" she asked, wanting to stay but afraid if she did, she'd find herself squeezed ever more tightly between them.

Sabrina held onto Andy's hand as if it were her only link to reality. "Please stay, Hope. I'd like you to hear this, too." She squared her shoulders. She looked a little pale but mostly determined, and there were no traces of tears on her cheeks. "Trace—" Her voice held a hard edge.

"Before you go on," Trace inserted smoothly, "I'd like to say a couple of things myself."

It was a masterful interruption, completely derailing his sister's train of thought. "But—I—" Bree glanced at Andy as if for guidance.

Trace didn't give her a chance to marshal her thoughts or her forces. "If Andy still wants me to be his best man, I'm pleased to accept." His irresistible smile flashed. "And I've had another inspiration, based on the success of tonight's shindig. I think we should hire Celebrations to plan the wedding."

His smile grew broader in the face of their universal astonishment. "I see I have your interest."

Hope thought she heard a wicked expectation in his tone. Very clever, she had to admit. He doubtless believed he could afford a generous gesture because he still didn't believe the wedding would ever take place.

"Now," he announced in a tone that said he figured he had them all eating out of his hand, "what was it you wanted to talk to me about, Sabrina?"

There followed a moment of stunned silence, and then Sabrina threw her arms around Hope. "Oh, please do it!" she cried. "We haven't even set the date and already I'm a wreck about this wedding. I was meaning to ask you myself but I didn't think I'd ever talk *him* into it."

Hope felt her hackles rise. Trace wanted the extravaganza of the century and Bree didn't, immediately putting anyone foolish enough to sign on as wedding consultant square dab in the middle of a brier patch. Hope didn't want the job, wasn't qualified to do the job, would under no circumstances take the job.

But hearing Bree express surprise that her brother would even consider Celebrations sure did set Hope's teeth on edge. She couldn't help glaring at Trace over his sister's shoulder.

Sabrina babbled on. "I was afraid he'd hire some big ritzy wedding consultant who'd want to stage the ceremony in Texas Stadium and fly in the Vienna Boys' Choir for a half-time show. But if *you* do it, I know it'll be okay. Please, Hope, please, please, please say you will!"

Andy looked equally relieved. "Damn! That's a great idea." He seemed to take it as settled and turned to Trace. "About that best man business—"

Hope held her breath, and she thought Trace might be doing the same, although his expression never changed. She had no idea what was coming but she wouldn't blame Andy if he handed Trace his walking papers.

Instead, Andy broke into a tight smile and thrust out his hand. "Of course, the invitation still stands. Thanks, Trace. Sabrina and I appreciate it."

The two men shook hands. Hope didn't know how Andy could do it, but he did.

Sabrina tried to draw Hope toward a couch. "We have so much to talk about," she bubbled. "Dates, guest lists, gowns—"

"Wait a minute." Andy looked from Bree to Trace. "We came in here to say something to your brother," he reminded her. "Don't you think—"

She tensed and all the happiness fled from her face.

Hope squeezed Bree's hands and gave her a searching look. "Why don't you save that for later?" she suggested. "You and Andy should see to your guests. After the party's over, there'll be plenty of time to talk."

"Good Lord, that's right." Automatically Bree reached up to smooth her blond hair. "How rude of me. Let's go down, Andy." She took his hand and started toward the door, never so much as glancing at her brother. Apparently all was not yet sweetness and light.

Trace scowled after them. "She's mad at me, all right." He gave Hope a searching glance. "What do you suppose Andy's going to do about the job? Will he take it?"

"Search me." She had no intention of letting him off the hook, even had it been in her power.

His glance narrowed. "Meaning, you wouldn't tell me if you knew. You won't even speculate?"

"That's right."

"How about the wedding? Will Celebrations take it on? I know you can answer that."

"I can." She smiled sweetly. "But I won't."

Head high, she swept past him, out the door and down the stairs. This was the first time she'd bested him but she didn't feel any particular joy of victory.

In fact, she found herself wondering if she'd live to regret it.

* * *

As it turned out, the next week was almost gone before the four of them found a mutually agreeable time to get together. Whatever Andy and Sabrina still had to say, they weren't about to give it away before they were ready. Neither Trace nor Hope had any luck trying to extract information.

At Andy's suggestion, they agreed to meet at a restaurant for dinner and conversation. "Neutral territory," he'd confided to Hope.

Trace volunteered to pick Hope up at Celebrations and drive her to the restaurant, which was one of the most elegant in Dallas. "It'll also give me a chance to weasel a little information out of you in advance," he'd confided.

So here she was, uncomfortably seated in the luxurious sports car, trying to hold herself aloof and give nothing away while Trace badgered her for information through heavy traffic on the Stemmons Expressway. Andy and Sabrina had chosen a Dallas landmark, the fifty-story Reunion Tower with its restaurant and revolving lounge. Appropriate, Hope, who had never been there, thought dryly. We'll have an excuse if anybody gets sick to their stomach during these negotiations.

"—so Bree's avoided me like the plague ever since the party," Trace was saying, "and I haven't even seen Andy. Do you know what they've decided about the job?"

"No, and I don't want to know until they're ready to tell me," she said staunchly.

"What are you doing, trying to make me look bad?" He steered the car onto the Commerce Street and Reunion Boulevard exit. He darted her a quick, guarded glance. "Okay, moving right along to the next crisis— Will Celebrations take on this wedding?''

She'd known this was coming and had prepared for it. "I'm ready to put you out of your misery on that point," she informed him. "No, Celebrations will *not* handle this wedding."

He looked elaborately crushed. "I didn't pay you enough for the engagement party," he guessed gloomily. "The bill was so low that I knew you'd given me a discount but Sabrina said—"

"Trace!" She couldn't let him think that, when, in fact, he'd doubled the bill and delivered a check in person. He'd paid her enough to keep Celebrations afloat for another two months, all by himself. "You were very generous and I appreciated it, but—"

"I can be a hell of a lot more generous than that." He flashed that irresistible grin, then turned back to traffic problems.

Hope stared out the window, biting her lip against a sigh. Why did she think Trace was talking about more than money?

Cocktails at the Top of the Dome were pleasant. Dinner at the Antares, one level down, was delicious, which meant that dessert was bound to turn serious. Throughout the meal, Trace seemed to grow more and more wary, apparently determined to let Andy and Sabrina take the lead.

Which Hope, for one, thought was darned nice of him. Knowing his penchant for control, such restraint couldn't be easy for him.

When the cheesecake was served and the coffee warmed, Andy cleared his throat ostentatiously, quickly drawing everyone's attention.

"First of all," he said in a tone so sincere it could not be doubted, "Sabrina and I want to thank both of you for that great party Saturday. To Trace and Hope."

He lifted his wineglass and drank, and they all followed suit—Hope uncomfortably. She wasn't sure she liked having her name linked with Trace's, even in a toast.

"Next," Andy continued as if reading off an agenda only he could see, "I want you both to know that Bree and I agree I should take the job in California."

Hope gasped and shot an alarmed glance at Trace. Could the others see the faint quickening of the pulse throbbing at his throat, the quick flare in his eyes?

She leaned forward earnestly. "Really, Bree? You don't mind?"

Bree's mouth turned down petulantly at the corners. "Oh, I mind all right," she said, "but Andy thinks—" She leaned against his shoulder with a rueful smile. "Andy says it's for our future and I know he's right. What's a little ol' separation when we'll have the rest of our lives together? He'll come here on weekends, I can go there—"

"That's wonderfully mature of you," Hope praised, her choice of words as much for Trace's benefit as for his sister's.

Bree made a face. "Yes, isn't it?" she agreed, glaring at her brother, who to this point had revealed little and said less.

"It wasn't an easy decision," Andy put in, his gaze locking with that of his future brother-in-law, "since there's no possibility of Sabrina joining me until she fulfills her teaching contract in June. But it's a good career move for me and we want to thank Trace for putting in a good word—getting the ball rolling, so to speak."

"Yes, thanks so much, big brother!" Sabrina's eyes flashed.

Andy patted her arm, perhaps in warning. But if either of them thought they'd be putting Trace on the defensive, they had to be disappointed. He merely dipped his chin in acknowledgment.

"No thanks are necessary," he said. "Anytime I can be of assistance I'm glad to do it."

"That's what worries me," Bree shot back.

"All right," Hope put in, figuring it was time to head off another major blowup, "with that decided, what about a wedding date?"

She held her breath. She thought Trace did, too. Sabrina turned an agonized face toward her fiancé, but he shook his head in a gentle warning.

Bree gave Andy the briefest of nods. "June fifteen," she said shortly, "if I can stand it that long."

Trace nodded, satisfaction barely visible in his expression. "Sounds good," he said in a completely neutral tone. "Hope, will that give Celebrations enough time to—"

"I told you, Celebrations can't possibly handle an event of this magnitude—"

"You've got to!" Bree leaned forward beseechingly. "I won't be able to stand it if you don't!"

"Cuz, I'd take it as a personal favor if you'd reconsider."

"Please, everybody!" Hope spread her hands in entreaty. "This job is too big!"

Trace joined the fray against her. "It's unanimous, Hope. Only *you* can make this happen—a dream wedding, the kind of wedding any woman would want."

"Whose dream, Trace?" Sabrina demanded. "Yours or mine?" Andy might have calmed her down but she obviously wasn't past her resentment.

"Yours, honey." He sounded unexpectedly melancholy, and unbearably loving. "I thought every woman dreamed of her wedding day. I know—" He stopped short, his face suddenly vulnerable, but just for a second, then he went on more briskly. "Anything my sister wants—sky's the limit. Six white horses and a golden carriage..."

Sabrina's surprise and delight were evident. "Oh, Trace," she groaned, "why do I let you do this to me?"

"Damn!" Andy looked perplexed. "You don't really want six white horses? I said I'd go along with anything that made you happy but that might be a tad much, even in Texas."

Sabrina laughed. Like magic, the mood at the table lightened. "It's a family joke," she explained. "When I was a little girl, I used to say I'd have a golden coach and six white horses someday. And Trace used to say he'd make sure I did."

"And a handsome prince?" Hope prompted around the lump in her throat. "That's the most important part."

"That's the part I've already got," Sabrina agreed. Her hostility had been swept away in a single stroke and she spoke with an openness that couldn't be questioned or ignored. "Trace, it wouldn't take much to convince me that Andy and I would be better off with a quick trip to a justice of the peace—not elopement, just two people getting married."

"Don't," he said, his voice husky. "Don't do that to me, Sabrina. But most of all, don't do it to yourself."

For a moment, brother and sister connected, and they were alone in that communion. At last, Sabrina sighed.

"Okay, barring that, I can understand the necessity for a big wedding, especially after seeing how many people we had to invite to the engagement party. But that concession made, I want it perfectly clear that I won't have a lot of time to worry about this. Between teaching and traveling to spend time with my handsome prince and getting ready to move to California as soon as school's out and we're married, I'm not going to be available at the drop of a hat."

"That," he said positively, "is why we need Hope."

Hope blinked. She'd considered herself out of this. "Hey," she objected, "that's not fair!"

"You're absolutely right." Sabrina ignored Hope's protests to speak to Trace. "She can make all those little decisions that I don't have time to be bothered with. Why not? I trust her like a sister."

"Wait a minute—"

Trace grinned at Bree. "And you trust me like a brother. Perfect. Hope and I can pull this wedding together, no problem." He turned in his seat and took Hope's cold hand. "What do you say? Do it for Sabrina. Do it for your cousin." He squeezed her hand. "Do it for me."

"But—but..." She clamped her mouth shut. Why argue? She knew she'd end up doing it. It wasn't possible to resist the appeals of three—make that two people she loved and one who scared the dickens out of her.

Andy took the job and two weeks later flew to California. Before he left, Sabrina was too intent upon spending every available minute with him to talk to Hope about the wedding. After he left, she was too depressed and distracted to care, she insisted.

No matter what Hope mentioned, Sabrina would only sigh and say, "Whatever you think is best."

"That's all well and good," Hope was finally moved to reply in mid-April, "after you make a few basic decisions. For starters, where do you want this wedding to be held? In a church? A country club? A hotel? Where? We've already run out of time to get reservations, Bree, unless somebody else cancels."

Bree was curled up in a tight little ball of misery on a window seat in the sitting room of her elegant turquoise and white bedroom suite at the Flying M. Now her eyes misted with tears, and she hugged a tapestry cushion to her bosom as if it was keeping her afloat. "I don't care. Ask Trace."

Hope tried not to convey the dismay she felt. She made a notation on her clipboard. "Okay, talk to Trace about a site. Now about your gown. You'll have to get involved in that."

"Oh. Oh, yes. I suppose so."

"Well?" Hope nudged. "Shall I do a little preliminary scouting and report back to you?"

"Sure, if you want to."

"*Want* to? With a million other details piling up? I'm here to help," she soothed. "Okay, attendants' gowns. How many bridesmaids would you like? What colors—"

"Please, not now." Bree rested her cheek on the cushion in her arms.

"But—"

"You're the maid of honor. What color do you like?"

"Emerald green, I guess, but—"

"Then the attendants will wear emerald green. Wasn't that easy?"

Hope had to laugh. "Unfortunately, that's not the way it's done. My dream wedding may be entirely different from yours."

"Not so far." Bree gave Hope a measuring look. "You know, we're just about the same size, you and me."

Hope looked down at herself—ugh, faded jeans were one thing but she really should replace this old pair—and then at Sabrina, serene and beautiful in navy linen. But Bree was right—beneath the surface decoration, they were approximately the same size. "Six in good stuff, eight in cheap?" Hope guessed.

Sabrina laughed. "Six is usually about right."

Hope felt her cheeks warm. Sabrina didn't wear cheap stuff. "Okay, so we're about the same size. Am I missing some hidden significance to that?"

"Just that in a pinch, you could try on wedding gowns for me, even go to fittings."

Hope was aghast. "But wouldn't that be bad luck or something? I thought only the bride should try on the gown before the wedding day."

"No, no, the groom's not supposed to see the bride in her wedding gown before the ceremony. That's what you're thinking of."

"Maybe so, but I still don't think it would be right," Hope objected primly. "However, I'm sure it won't come to that."

Trace wandered through the open door. He wore jeans almost as faded as Hope's and a camel-colored sweater that could only be cashmere. His hair was wet, as if he'd just climbed out of a shower. "How's it going?" he asked.

"Fine," Sabrina said listlessly.

"Awful," Hope said helplessly. "Bree, you've got to give me some parameters, here."

"Such as?" Trace pulled up a huge, round hassock covered in robin's egg blue and sat down. His interest was in direct proportion to Sabrina's lack of same.

"Such as where the ceremony will be held."

"Here," he said promptly.

"Here?" Sabrina and Hope repeated simultaneously.

"Sure. We're talkin' June, right?"

"Right." They both nodded.

"So we'll have the wedding in the garden. We can put up some of those big tents, open the house for the reception."

"A garden wedding!" Hope closed her eyes, seeing the Flying M garden in full bloom, seeing the surrounding grounds green and alive—

She hoped it was Sabrina's dream because it had just become hers.

She opened her eyes and found Trace staring at her. When she caught him at it, he turned his attention to his sister.

Sabrina looked thoughtful. Finally she said, "Yeah, that would work. Okay, a garden wedding it is. If it's okay with you, Hope. Do you foresee any problems?"

"Oh, no problems," Hope said, grateful they'd apparently missed her initial unseemly burst of enthusiasm. This was, after all, Sabrina's wedding.

Trace turned all that Morgan charm on Hope. "There, that's settled. We'll have the ceremony and reception right here. I'm on a problem-solving roll. What's next?"

"Well..." She chewed on the end of her pencil, her mind racing over all the reading she'd been doing lately about how to survive a wedding. "The gown, I guess. Sabrina would like me to narrow down possibilities—is that right, Bree?—to save time. I thought I might go to a few bridal salons—"

Trace was shaking his head, a stubborn slant to his mouth.

"Is there a problem?" Hope asked. Please don't let there be another problem!

"They'll come to you."

"Who'll come to me?"

"The bridal salons. Just call 'em and tell 'em when you want them here and they'll load everything up and come a-runnin'.''

"Are you serious?''

"Hell, yes! Just tell them the bride will be Sabrina Morgan and doors hitherto closed will open like magic." He had that look in his eyes that could be teasing...or maybe not. "But I might have an even better idea." He pursed his lips thoughtfully. "I met a designer a couple of years ago and she might whip up something special, if you'd like to give her a call. Or I could do it, if you're shy."

"I am *not* shy," Hope prevaricated with dignity. She was thinking, *Designer*?

Sabrina frowned. "Are you talking about May McAngel?"

Hope gasped. Even she, who was not exactly au courant in the wonderful world of fashion, knew May McAngel's Heavenly label.

Trace nodded, watching Hope. The familiar tug of a smile at the corner of his mouth warned her he'd seen through her yet again.

After an initial moment of enthusiasm, Sabrina shook her head. "No. She'd ask me a lot of questions about what I like and don't like and I'm in no mood to like anything. I mean, how do I know what kind of wedding gown I want? When I see it, I'll know. Or Hope will. Who cares, so long as it's white?"

"Oh, Sabrina!" Hope groaned and fell back against the cushions. "Here you are, in a position any other bride-to-be would kill for—pardon the simile. In a position that would make any other bride-to-be think she'd died and gone to heaven—oops.''

Sabrina looked puzzled but Trace was openly laughing at Hope's efforts to make a point. She gave him a sheepish grin.

"Let me try one more time. You're moping around as if the world was about to come to an end, when you should be the happiest woman on earth. You're engaged to a wonderful man who adores you, and you have a golden opportunity to make your dream wedding come true. Any other woman would be jumping for joy!''

Trace cocked his head. "Would you?'' he asked Hope.

"Well, of course. I'm only human. Unfortunately, I'm not engaged and I'll certainly never have a wedding like—'' Sudden inspiration struck her. She knew how to get Sabrina's cooperation. "Bree, I'll never have an opportunity to plan a wedding like this for myself. But I'll take so much pleasure in making it perfect—'' cross those fingers behind her back, she'd strive for perfect but settle for wonderful ''—for you and Andy. But I can't do it alone.''

Sabrina frowned, then slowly her brow cleared. Ah, thought Hope, it's going to work!

Sabrina stood up. "You won't have to do it alone,'' she said. "Trace will help you.''

And she drifted out of the room as if she were Camille looking for a likely place to expire.

CHAPTER SIX

HOPE stared at the guest list, finalized at five hundred—*five hundred people*! This was looking more like a coronation than a wedding. The thought of all that responsibility made her slightly nauseous.

So did the boxes of engraved wedding invitations, all waiting for her to address the envelopes. In calligraphy, yet. When would she ever find the time—

"Hire somebody," Trace ordered.

"What?"

She looked up from the heavy parchment invitation she held in her hand and into his blue, blue eyes. He seemed to fill her small shop with his presence.

"Hire somebody to address the invitations. That's what you were thinking about, isn't it?"

"Well, yes, but—"

"No buts, Hope. It's only a couple of months until this wedding and you don't have time to do everything yourself." He let his breath out impatiently. "I think we—you should hire someone to take up the slack while you concentrate on this. I'll be glad to—"

"Forget it, Trace." She shook her head vehemently. "I told you this was too big a job for me but you insisted. Now you're just going to have to let me do things my way."

His lean, handsome face hardened. "All right—for now. But if things start falling by the wayside—"

"They won't."

He nodded as if willing to give her the benefit of the doubt...this time. "Bring me up to date, then," he commanded. "How's it going? Any problems?"

She didn't bother to remind him that this was Bree and Andy's wedding, not his, and that they should be the ones receiving her report. Unfortunately for wedding planning purposes, Andy was in California and Bree was on a plane heading there for the weekend.

Not that Bree's presence would make Hope's job easier, since the bride-to-be was so distracted and miserable she couldn't seem to make a decision if her life depended on it. On the other hand, Trace was more than happy to make any and all decisions that came along. Hope didn't mind that so much as she minded the time she was forced to spend in his company.

To put it plainly, Mr. Trace Morgan drove her crazy! His sexy good looks and arrogant manner were almost more than plain little Hope Archer could deal with.

But she must try. "Okay," she said in her most businesslike tone, "I've spoken to Bree's bridesmaids and Andy's attendants and they all know what their duties will be. I've confirmed the date—June fifteen—and the time—three-thirty—with the judge, and that's all locked on."

"Good, good." He nodded approval. "What about the food, the cake, the photographer, the videographer, the florist, the musicians, the dress—"

"Stop!" She threw up her hands in alarm. "I'm talking to a photographer this afternoon but...you want a video, too?" She bit her lip. "I hadn't thought of that."

"You would have," he said brusquely. "I've taken the liberty of speaking to the manager of the Woodbriar Country Club about providing chefs—"

"Oh, thank you!" She'd had no idea where to turn for the food, since a meal as elaborate as the one he wanted was beyond the capabilities of the usual caterer.

"They'll do the cake, too. I said we'd go by there tomorrow morning for a tasting."

"A tasting—you and me? What about Bree?"

He arched one dark brow and his finely etched mouth curved into a faint smile. "What *about* Bree? Do you think she cares if the cake is lemon or chocolate? She told me to go ahead and do whatever I wanted."

Hope sighed. "She said the same thing to me about the flowers, but I thought she might change her mind."

"Don't count on it. I'll pick you up about ten tomorrow and we can go to the club together—why are you shaking your head?" He frowned at her.

"I can't do it tomorrow."

"And why not?" He did not look pleased.

"Because I've got a few last-minute details to take care of for another wedding."

"I see." His eyes narrowed. "That woman who was in here the day we met?"

"That's right." She was astonished he remembered. "Erlene's wedding is Saturday and I've got a slew of things to do, including finding someone to help with setting up and taking down chairs and tables and so on and so forth. The boy who usually helps me has a basketball tournament so—"

"I'll help you."

She stared at him openmouthed. "You'll *what*?"

"I'll help you. Hell, I can unfold a few chairs." He shrugged that objection away. "That settles it. Now you're free to go to that cake testing with me tomorrow morning."

He started toward the door.

"Wait!" He turned back, one eyebrow raised quizzically. She rushed on. "You don't know what you're saying. This is a fifties-themed wedding and everybody will be in costume, including me and—and whoever's helping out."

He frowned. "I thought this was the antebellum South wedding."

"You're a couple of themes late. After that she wanted King Arthur and now she's settled on the fifties."

He looked thoughtful, then nodded. "I can handle that. It's still settled."

"But—"

"I want to see you in action, Hope. It's settled!" And it was.

They agreed that the carrot cake was superb.

The pastry chef looked pleased by their enthusiasm. "I can make this in the shape of a basket overflowing with sugar flowers that look fresh-picked," he announced with obvious pride.

"Smaller matching basket cakes make great centerpieces for each table."

Trace looked at Hope. "What do you think?"

"Sounds good but—" She turned to the chef. "How much would it cost for—"

"Forget cost." Trace glowered at her. "Do you like it or don't you?"

"It's part of my *job* to remember costs," she reminded him. "I even signed a contract to that effect, remember?" He should—he'd insisted. She added, "And it's not whether I like it, it's how—"

"Hope, if you mention Sabrina's name one more time, I'll be tempted to—"

The baker cleared his throat. "You don't have to decide now," he said. "Let me make up a small sample for you to take to the bride. No rush."

Hope glanced at her wristwatch. "That's what you think," she said, adding, "thank you so much. That would be very helpful."

She followed Trace outside to his sports car. The air was April mild, the sun shining. Surely a good omen, Hope thought.

Trace opened the passenger door of the car. "Over lunch, you can bring me up to date on—"

"Oh, I'm sorry," she interrupted. "I thought you understood that I really have to get back to Celebrations. I have a meeting about an anniversary party in less than an hour."

He got that stormy look she was beginning to know too well. "I told Lillian we'd have lunch at the ranch."

She recoiled against the leather bucket seat. "You told Lillian that without mentioning it to me?"

"I saw no need. Hell, I'm giving you an entire Saturday so I just assumed—"

Hope groaned. "That's not fair. If I'd had a little warning—"

He slammed the car door on her words and she sat there unhappily until he'd climbed behind the steering wheel. She would *not* let him bully her this time!

He gave her a critical glance, then started the engine. "Can't Mrs. Casen fill in for you?"

"She might, but—"

"Dammit, Hope, why do you think I keep telling you to hire more help? We've got to decide about tents and landscaping and I've got all those people coming at two."

"I'm sorry. You should have checked with me first."

"No," he disagreed grimly, "what I should have done was what I wanted to do from the beginning—move you out to the ranch and keep you there for the duration."

"You're out of your mind! If you think I'm going to let my whole business go down the drain to placate you—"

"This wedding will *make* Celebrations, not send it down the drain. Pull this off and you'll be the hot new party planner of the hour, and you know it."

She didn't know it, not until he said it so baldly, and then she realized instantly that he was right. If only she didn't feel herself sailing farther and farther into uncharted waters. If she failed to make this wedding the social event of the year, she'd be taking Celebrations and the entire Archer clan down with her.

On the other hand, if she somehow managed to succeed—

He laughed, warm good humor returning. He sounded very much as if he knew he'd won. "We'll call Mrs. Casen from the ranch," he said. "She knows what a great opportunity this is for Celebrations. She won't mind a bit."

"All right," Hope agreed reluctantly, "but I just want you to know here and now that I will *not* move out to the ranch, so put it out of your mind."

The speculative glance he gave her did nothing to reassure her that he'd accepted her ultimatum.

They stood at the edge of the tennis courts—Hope and Trace, surrounded by representatives of the tent company, the landscapers, the lighting specialists and who knew how many others.

Trace touched Hope's hand lightly, as if to recall her from wherever her thoughts had flown. "So what do you think?" he asked, but gently, as if he realized how cowed she was by all this.

She gave him a quick, grateful smile. Everyone was looking at her and she simply wasn't up to the challenge. She'd open her mouth and make a fool of herself, she was sure of it.

But Trace was watching her, his expression encouraging and supportive. It was time to prove her worth as a wedding consultant, she realized, time to prove that Andy and Bree hadn't misplaced their faith.

"All right." Her voice came out crisp and filled with far more authority than she felt. "We want a fairy-tale wedding perfect in every detail, so this is what I see." She gestured to the tennis courts. "What if we tent that entire area and provide a canopied walkway from the house? I see the rest of the grounds as a fantasyland, brimming with tiny, twinkling lights—all clear, of course, not colored—and fresh flowers in marble planters everywhere."

The tent man nodded. "Sounds good, Ms. Archer. If we take down those nets—"

"Clear lights—good," the lighting man approved. "We can install indirect lighting at the base of some of the trees and flower urns—"

Conferring, the workers moved away to look over the area in minute detail. Hope was so relieved she almost slumped against Trace . . . or maybe she did, for she suddenly found his arm around her shoulder. She shivered at his touch but couldn't seem to draw away from the comfort he offered.

"W-was that all right?" she asked.

"Of course," he said blithely. "You're in charge."

She sighed, leaning a little more closely against his side. Amazing, how neatly she fit there. "Thank you. I do worry that I'll end up planning my own dream wedding instead of Sabrina's, though."

"Considering how little attention she's willing to give to this, perhaps that's for the best," he suggested grimly.

"Maybe, but it's also—" She bit off the word she'd been about to say—*dangerous*. This wedding was taking over her life. Or was it this man who was taking over?

"Also what?" He gave her a glance of pointed interest.

"Intimidating," she improvised. "It's intimidating to impose my tastes on someone else."

He laughed. "I don't see why. I do it all the time."

One of the workers called, and Trace released her and went to confer with the man. Hope suppressed a smile. One thing she really liked about Trace Morgan was that he still managed to retain a sense of humor, despite his arrogant ways.

One thing she liked? She sighed. Who was she kidding? There was very little about him she *didn't* like.

Trace and Hope lingered after the workers had gone. She gave him an oblique glance. "So are you satisfied with everything thus far?"

He nodded. "You? How's everything stacking up against your dream wedding?"

She laughed. "It's going to be far more extravagant than anything I could have imagined." She walked around a tennis net and to one side of the court. "This is where we should set up the altar, don't you think?"

He strolled after her, his expression considering. "Looks good, but maybe we'd better test it out."

"How do we do that?" she asked lightly, responding to what she took for teasing.

"Only one way I know," he said, reaching for her.

She was so shocked she simply stared at him with parted lips while he drew her into his embrace. Her head fell back to rest against his arm and still she looked into his face, piercingly aware of the sweetness of the moment.

His lips covered hers, lightly but with masterful purpose. She was lost. She slid her arms around his waist and closed her eyes, savoring his kiss and his nearness as if in a dream.

Too soon he lifted his head and stepped back, although he still held her with his hands on her upper arms. He looked at her with hooded eyes.

"Yes," he said.

"Y-yes?" She felt herself swaying and locked her knees.

"Yes, this is an excellent place to locate the altar. It passed *my* test. How about yours?"

"Absolutely." She tried to match her careless tone to his, as if the kiss meant nothing at all to her.

When, in fact, it had turned her world upside down.

Erlene Jones married Franklyn Webster Saturday afternoon in the recreation room of the mobile home park where they lived. In keeping with the fifties theme, the bride's daughter, the flower girl, wore a pink poodle skirt, matching pink blouse, dyed-to-match pink bobby sox and saddle shoes. The six bridesmaids and the maid of honor wore the same thing only in blue.

The bridegroom looked like an escapee from a motorcycle movie of the era—jeans, a torn T-shirt, leather biker boots and studded leather jacket, slicked-back hair and sunglasses.

Ah, but the bride...the bride outshone them all. Erlene walked down the aisle in a pleated white dress like the one Marilyn Monroe wore when she stood on a grate to let a passing subway train blow the skirt into immortality. Erlene had even bleached her hair for the occasion, and had it styled in a reasonable approximation of Marilyn's.

"And if you think it was easy to come up with that dress, think again," Hope whispered in an aside to Trace, who looked absolutely dumbfounded.

"I'll never underestimate you again," he whispered, "and that's a promise."

Nor would she underestimate him, not after the way he pitched in to help her make the wedding a success. He'd shown up on the dot, wearing faded jeans low on his hips, a white T-shirt under an open plaid sport shirt, loafers and white socks. His hair was plastered back with something he referred to as "greasy kid stuff."

He'd looked her over with obvious appreciation. "Nice," he said. "Very nice."

She'd blushed, standing there with her hair pulled back into a ponytail, wearing a gray cotton dress with a gathered skirt and matching pink bolero jacket. On her hands were short white gloves, on her feet, pink ballerina flats.

Mrs. Casen, who'd been the mother of teenagers in the fifties, had assured her that she had every detail just right, down to the small chiffon square tied at her throat.

She'd thought that once they went to work, she'd forget her assistant was the sexiest—not to mention wealthiest—man she'd ever met. She was wrong. Even as he willingly followed her instructions to set up the folding chairs over there, spread the tablecloths over here, she was achingly aware of him.

Once she'd sent the bride and all her attendants down the makeshift aisle, she'd had a few moments of respite during the actual ceremony. Standing next to Trace, she'd tried to act dignified, tried to seem untouched by the occasion, but it was impossible. No sooner had the minister begun to speak than she choked up. Fat tears slid down her cheeks and she choked back sobs.

Trace stared at her, his expression apprehensive. "You okay?" he whispered.

She swallowed hard and nodded, dabbing at her wet cheeks with one gloved finger. "Weddings do this to me," she confessed. "I can't help it. It's so beautiful when two people pledge their lives to each other—"

She couldn't go on. As if he understood, Trace slid one arm across her quaking shoulder and gave her a hug. And as the ceremony was ending, he produced a handkerchief and gently dried her wet cheeks.

Hope might have burst into tears again at his tenderness had not duty called. While Trace made sure the caterer was putting everything in the correct place, Hope dashed off to help the photographer get the shots he needed of the wedding party. By the time she made it back to the reception area, Trace had everything in apple-pie order.

Hope paused beside one of the two bars set up on opposite sides of the room. The bartender sidled up to her.

"Man, I don't know where you got that guy but he is *good*!" the man said admiringly. "Lone Star Liquors sent over the wrong assortment and I thought we were in for it. But that guy whipped out orders like he was Napoleon or something and within fifteen minutes we had exactly what we'd ordered—and I mean *exactly*. Man, I am major impressed!''

Hope was, too. Trace was the kind of man you'd want on your side in any crisis or emergency.

Accompanied by applause, Erlene the bride and Franklyn the bridegroom reappeared. The photographer gave Hope a thumbs-up, raised his camera and went back to work. The happy newlyweds made their way slowly across the crowded room to where Hope and Trace stood.

Erlene threw her arms around her wedding consultant. "Honey, I can't thank you enough," she exclaimed. "Everything's just perfect! You and your helper—" She smiled at Trace. "Well, you two made all the difference."

Franklyn fished a business card out of his jeans pocket and thrust it at Trace. "I keep hearin' how you set them old boys from the liquor store straight. I got me a small construction company and I can always use a good man. You gimme a call if you're ever lookin' for work."

Hope stared at Franklyn, aghast. In all good faith, he was offering work to a man who could buy him and sell him a thousand times over. Holding her breath, she turned to Trace.

He examined the business card. "Construction, huh?" He looked at Franklyn with an easy smile. "Maybe we can do business one of these days." He slipped the card in a hip pocket. "Can I get you some champagne? Looks like the toasts are about to begin."

"Followed by the sock hop!" Erlene sang out as her new husband hauled her off toward the dance floor where the bridal party was assembling. "You two relax and enjoy yourselves now, you hear? You deserve it!"

They might deserve it but they didn't get it, with so much to be done to keep everything running smoothly. They did manage one dance, but only because Trace insisted.

In fact, he almost dragged Hope onto the dance floor. The band struck up an old Elvis Presley ballad and he hauled her into his arms, leading her through a quick series of steps before settling into the rhythm of the song. By then, she was breathless...or maybe she'd been breathless before.

"You know what?" he murmured against her hair.

"No, what?" She wished he wouldn't hold her so closely, her head tucked just beneath his chin. They fit together so naturally that it was scary. She could learn to like this...a lot.

He curved one hand around her neck and pressed her cheek against his chest. "You look so prim and proper in your ponytail and your little white gloves that I almost feel bad trying to lead you astray...on the dance floor, I mean."

"Y-you should feel bad. I'm supposed to be working," she said breathlessly.

"You take your responsibilities very seriously, don't you."

She found him so easy to follow in the most intricate steps that she found herself wishing the music would never end. With an effort, she pulled her thoughts to his comment. "Of course I take my work seriously. Don't you—take your work seriously, I mean."

"Too seriously, I've been told. Recently I've begun to wonder if my critics could be right. All work and no play—"

"You couldn't be a dull boy if you tried for a month of Sundays," she burst out.

"Thanks for your vote of confidence," he drawled. "But I've just about decided to take some time away from the company. I don't remember my last vacation, so I'm due."

Her heart stopped beating. "You wouldn't go away before the wedding!" Without him, she'd be lost.

"Are you kidding? We're in this together, girl, and it's going to take both of us to pull it off."

Relief, blessed relief, flowed through her. "Then I don't understand."

"Simple." He moved his hand in a small, sensuous circle at the small of her back. "I think I proved here today that we work very well together. If I can't get you to hire a full-time assistant, maybe I should take on the job myself."

"You're kidding, of course." A spark of apprehension shot down her spine. "You're kidding, right?"

Before he could answer, the music ended. He did not, however, release her from his embrace, even when the bride announced that it was time to throw the bouquet.

He loosened his hold only enough to let her lift her face so he could see her expression. "Do I look like I'm kidding?" he asked softly.

"N-no." She tried to wiggle out of his arms and only succeeded in bringing her hips more fully against his. "But you must be!"

"I don't kid," he said flatly. "I say what I mean. I also meant it when I said I want you to move out to the ranch until it's all over."

"No!" She braced her palms against his chest. "I can't do that."

"Of course you can, if you'll hire someone to assist Mrs. Casen in your absence."

"I can't afford—"

"I phrased that poorly. You'll do the hiring but I'll foot the bill. I want you to devote all your time to making Sabrina's big day a success, and I'm willing to pay to get what I want."

"You make me feel as if . . . as if you're trying to buy *me*," she said with distaste. "I'm not for sale, Mr. Morgan."

"Everything's for sale, Miss Archer—and every-*body*, if the price is right."

"That's a despicable attitude!"

Wrenching herself free of his light hold, she whirled. Something struck her shoulder, and instinctively she threw out her hands.

The bridal bouquet plopped into them, and Hope stared at it dumbly. A shriek of approval brought her head swinging up again.

"Oh, my gosh," she exclaimed, looking around frantically for someone to whom she could hand off the bouquet. She didn't want to horn in on the festivities this way. She wasn't even a guest!

But it was Erlene, the bride herself, who had let out a whoop of approval. "Way to go, Hope!" She waved from across the dance floor. "You'll be the next bride, mark my words!"

The only thing Hope wanted to be next for was to sink through the floor and straight into oblivion.

Trace settled into the driver's seat of the sports car and grinned at Hope over his shoulder. "My favorite part," he announced, "was the money dance."

Hope slumped in her seat with a groan, clutching the bridal bouquet on her lap. She'd begged Erlene to throw it again, explained over and over that she'd only caught it on a fluke. Nobody had paid the slightest attention to her protests, however.

Now the festivities were over and she was exhausted, and a whole lot more—happy because everything had turned out the way Erlene wanted it, miserable because Trace had thrown her off stride and kept her there.

She tried to concentrate on what he was saying. "The money dance? Why?"

"Because I never saw anything like it before. All the men dancing with the bride and pinning money on her dress, the women dancing with the groom and pinning money on his shirt. It was, to say the very least, *strange*."

She sighed. "I thought so, too, the first time I saw it. But it's really kind of fun, and helps pay for the honeymoon at the same time. I thought you might find it... you know, crass or something."

"Crass? Hell, I loved it." He steered out of the parking lot. "I loved it so much I pinned a five-hundred-dollar bill on her."

"You didn't! She'll go crazy trying to figure out where that came from."

"Yeah." His eyes held a mischievous twinkle. "I had a swell time today, Hope. Thanks for taking me along."

"You're entirely welcome," she said, not meaning it. He'd been a great help to her, as far as the work went, but he'd also kept her nerves on edge and her pulse racing, neither of which she wanted or needed.

He shot her a narrow glance. "Say what you really mean. You're angry with me."

"I am not!" But she said it angrily.

"You are. You're angry because I want all your time and attention. You think I'm selfish."

"I am *not* angry." She bit her lip. "Okay, a little bit. But I don't *think* you're selfish, I know it. I can't walk away from my business and devote myself to nothing but making you happy!" *But oh! I'd like to*, she realized, a thought that frightened her.

"Is that how it seems? Sorry, but it has nothing to do with making me happy."

"Oh, come now!"

"It has to do with making Sabrina happy. And of course, if she's happy, then Andy will be, too."

She felt as if she'd been ambushed. "That's not fair," she objected. "Sabrina doesn't care anything about this wedding, she only cares about getting married."

"That's how it seems," he agreed, "but is it, really? Don't you think she may wake up some morning and realize that she wants this very much indeed?"

"W-why, I don't know—"

"Hope, if it were left up to me, there wouldn't be a wedding or a marriage or any other damned thing between my sister and your cousin. You know that, don't you?"

She'd hoped against hope that he'd changed his mind, but here he was, bluntly telling her that he felt exactly the same way he had at the beginning. She nodded miserably.

He stared straight ahead at the road instead of at her. "If she's determined to marry this guy, I'm going to give her the best send-off I possibly can," he said in a hard voice. "There'll be no sneaking around, no whispers, no split in the family. As far as the rest of the world will know, I'll be one hundred percent in favor of the match."

He braked at a stop light and pinned her to her seat with his glance. "If that's selfish, so be it."

"It doesn't sound selfish to me," Hope whispered.

"Good." Eyes gleaming with satisfaction, he accelerated through the green light. "So how quickly can you hire someone? The sooner we get you moved out to the ranch, the sooner we can get a handle on this wedding."

CHAPTER SEVEN

THE thought of living under the same roof with Trace Morgan petrified Hope, so she stalled.

She couldn't find anyone to fill in for her at Celebrations, she told him. Yes, she was advertising, she was interviewing, but he could hardly expect the perfect person to walk in off the street and—

The perfect person walked in off the street. Her name was Lisa Peters and she was forty-three years old, had ten years experience with a florist and another three in charge of children's parties for a theme park in California. For the last year and a half she'd been working for a large catering company right here in Dallas but now wanted something with a little more flexibility.

She was perfect. She was even willing to work for what Hope could afford to pay, and was prepared to start immediately. And the capper was, Mrs. Casen liked her.

Trace called the next day and Hope reluctantly gave him the news that she'd hired someone.

"So when can you be packed?" he asked impatiently. "I can pick you up in a couple of hours if—"

"Look," she said, steeling herself, "I'm willing to give this wedding one hundred percent of my time but I simply can't move out to the ranch."

There was a pause, and then he said, his voice cold as crystal, "And why not, may I ask?"

"I...I just wouldn't feel right about it." That much was certainly true.

"Would you care to explain that?"

"Not...really. I just wouldn't."

"Are you under the impression that you're so irresistible I won't be able to forgo the temptation?"

Her cheeks flamed. Thank goodness they were having this conversation over the telephone. "Certainly not!"

"Then what is it? It's not as if we were going to be alone. Sabrina will be here, and Lillian's quarters are in the main house. If I ever lose my head and put the moves on you—"

"You know that's not what I meant," she objected miserably. No, what she'd meant was, she was afraid she might lose her head and put the moves on *him*, in which case it wouldn't matter how many people were in the house because nobody would be calling for help. "I'm sorry, Trace, I really am, but I can't do it."

There was a long pause, and then he said coolly, "All right, Hope. I won't ask again."

Thank God, she thought, hanging up with a heavy heart. Trace Morgan must be the hardest man in the world to say no to.

And even harder to make that no stick. Thirty minutes later, Sabrina called. "Hope, Hope, I've got the most wonderful idea! Why don't you move out here to the ranch to work on the wedding? If you're nearby, I might even be able to keep from slitting my wrists before the great day arrives! Isn't that fabulous? I don't know why I didn't think of it before. Of course, I had to talk Trace into it but after the way I've been moping around, I guess he was ready to agree to anything. So when can you come, Hope? Please, please, please come right away! With you here, I might survive until... until..." And she burst into tears.

Hope moved to the Flying M the next morning. So much for standing firm.

Without a single "I told you so," Trace assigned her to a suite of rooms that included a bedroom and an office-sitting room with desk and computer from which she could plan the wedding in comfort and with maximum efficiency. When Lillian took Hope up, her luggage was already there, stacked just inside the door on the pearl gray rug.

"It's beautiful," she gasped, turning slowly to survey the sunny room brightened by east-facing windows. From candy-striped yellow and white wallpaper to cushy yellow upholstered furniture and polished woods, the room glowed.

"Glad you like it, honey." Lillian picked up a case. She seemed as friendly as Hope remembered, if perhaps a bit distracted. "You'll like the bedroom, too. Right this way."

Hope did like it. An antique canopy bed stood on a platform in the middle of the room, an intricately pieced quilt used for a covering. Every detail contributed to the feeling of old-time elegance.

"Think you'll be comfortable in here?" Lillian asked. "Because if you're not, Trace said to—"

"But this is wonderful! I've never even seen such a wonderful bedroom."

It was the truth. Although she hadn't exactly spent her life to date sitting in the cinders, Hope couldn't help feeling more like Cinderella than Friday's child as she surveyed her elegant new surroundings. For once someone else was doing the giving...

She even knew where to find her handsome prince. But without a glass slipper to her name, it seemed unlikely that he'd ever mistake her for a princess.

Lillian lifted a suitcase onto the bed. "Let me help you unpack."

Was her voice trembling? Hope frowned. "That's not necessary," she said, sliding an arm around the older woman's shoulders. "What is it, Lillian? You seem upset."

The housekeeper bit her lip. "My goodness, and here I was thinkin' I was hiding it so well."

"Hiding what?" Hope drew the woman to a chintz-covered settee. "You're upset. Can I help?"

Lillian's smile was tremulous, and she sighed. "My daughter in Florida called last night to tell me she's going into the hospital day after tomorrow for..." She swallowed hard. "Some tests...and a biopsy. She says it's routine, but..." She twisted her apron between her hands.

"But you'd like to see for yourself."

Lillian shook her head ruefully. "It's easy to see why Sabrina's so crazy about you, Hope. I know I'm being silly—"

"Nothing's silly if it springs from love."

"Amen to that." Lillian drew a shaky breath. "I feel better just talking about it."

"You haven't told Bree or Trace?"

The housekeeper shook her head. "Trace has been an ol' bear lately, and Bree—well, she's goin' out of her mind over being separated from Andy. I didn't want to bother them, what with everything in such an uproar."

Hope spoke sternly. "Lillian, tell Trace. He would want you to be with your family at a time like this."

"I know you're right. Maybe..."

"No maybe about it. Promise me you will."

Lillian's smile seemed to come a bit easier. "I promise I'll do what needs doin'." She leaned forward to give Hope a quick hug. "It was a great day for all of us when you came to this house, Hope Archer. I, for one, hope you never leave!"

Trace did not appear for dinner that night, to Hope's simultaneous relief and disappointment. "He often works late," Sabrina explained. "When I'm alone, I usually eat off a tray in my room. But with you here—" She gave Hope a brilliant smile.

So her presence was already making a difference for Bree, Hope thought, relaxing a little. Perhaps Trace was right, perhaps this was for the best.

She continued thinking so right up until she started to ascend the sweeping staircase on her way to bed that first night. With her foot on the third step, the tall front door swung open and Trace walked into the foyer.

He saw her and stopped dead in his tracks. For a moment he stared at her and then his gaze lifted to the top of the stairs—where the bedrooms lay, she suddenly found herself thinking. Her cheeks warmed.

His smile didn't erase the lines of strain on his face. He looked tired, and she longed to offer some sort of comfort and solace.

"I'm glad you're here," he said simply. "We'll do our best to see you don't regret coming."

Turning, he walked across the foyer, through the doorway and out of sight. Only then did Hope let out the breath she'd been holding.

Dealing with this man on her own turf had been tricky. Dealing with him on his would likely prove to be…impossible. Sighing, she walked up the stairs to bed.

Hope hurried downstairs the next morning to join Sabrina for breakfast before she had to rush off to school. Over juice and coffee and a basket of muffins and pastries, the two had their first really significant communication about the wedding.

Happily, Hope discovered that she and Bree really did have much the same taste about details such as dresses and music, food and flowers.

"I don't know why you're so surprised," Bree said impishly. "I've had faith in you all along."

"And in your brother," Hope added. "Sometimes I think he's taken more of an interest than you have."

Bree thrust out her lower lip petulantly. "It's not that I'm not interested, Hope."

"I know. You've been so busy—"

"That's not the reason." Bree looked up with stormy blue eyes very like her brother's.

"Then what is?"

"It's…Andy."

"Andy doesn't want a big wedding?" Hope was astonished. She'd been sure Andy was willing to go along with anything his bride-to-be wanted.

Bree shook her head. "It's not that. I'm afraid he'll get tired of waiting for me, get tired of all this hassle, get tired of putting up with Trace."

"I think Trace has been very reasonable," Hope said staunchly. Honesty made her add, "Lately, anyway."

"It's an act," Bree said flatly.

"Oh, surely you're mistaken. He's reconciled to the marriage, Bree, and he's doing everything he can to make the wedding perfect for you."

"Perfect for Andy would have been a justice of the peace two months ago." Her mouth trembled. "Don't you see, he's in California without me! He's making new friends, a new life, and here I am, still part of the old. I want to be with him!"

"He wants that, too." Hope felt close to tearing up herself. "It looks to me as if you're beginning to doubt his love just a tiny little bit."

"Never!" Her eyes flew wide. "All I doubt is the wisdom of waiting so very, very long."

Hope reached across the table to squeeze Bree's hand. "Too late to worry about that—and believe me, if you were doing the planning you'd realize how little time there really is. Speaking of which, you have absolutely got to pick your wedding gown. Until you do, I can't pin down the florist or the cake or much of anything."

"You poor little thing, I don't mean to cause you so much trouble." Bree gave Hope's hand a squeeze and jumped up. "Look, I'll try to get a substitute to fill in for me Monday. Why don't you see if you can set something up then?'' She glanced at her wristwatch. ''I'm late. I'll see you tonight, okay?'' Blowing a kiss, she headed for the door.

She brushed past Trace on her way out. ''See you later, big brother,'' she called without slowing her pace.

Sitting at the long shiny table, Hope tried a tentative smile. She wished Bree had stayed longer or that Trace had come down earlier, so she wouldn't have to be alone with him her first morning in his house. She took comfort from knowing he had his own busy day ahead and would doubtless leave soon after breakfast.

He poured himself a cup of coffee from the sideboard and sat across the table from her. His somber gaze made her want to squirm but she forced herself to sit quietly.

After what seemed an eternity, he spoke. ''Is everything here satisfactory, Hope?''

''More than satisfactory.'' She stared at her English muffin for a moment. ''I...I'm sorry I raised such a fuss about coming here.'' She looked up suddenly. ''Do you ever get the feeling that some things are just meant to be?''

''Why—'' He looked startled. ''I'm not sure I know what you mean.''

''Well, like my new employee showing up out of the blue like she did. Bree needed me, I see that now, but I'd dug in my heels. If the absolutely perfect employee hadn't shown up—'' She shrugged, then brightened. ''All's well that ends well, I suppose. I just want you to know that you were right and I was wrong and I'm very glad to be here. Now I can devote all my time to making Sabrina's wedding day perfect.''

"Hope Archer," he said slowly, "sometimes I don't believe you." His blue eyes warmed and his mouth curved into a smile.

His approval brought a flush of pleasure to her cheeks and a warm glow throughout the rest of her. Trace Morgan was a powerful man, a difficult man at times, but he was also a man with charisma to burn.

"If that's a compliment," she said breathlessly, "thank you. If it's not, don't tell me."

He laughed. "I'm not even sure, myself, about that. But I am sure about one thing—Sabrina went out of here this morning happier than I've seen her in I don't know how long, thanks to you." He glanced around. "Have you had breakfast?"

She nodded. "I was just about to go up and get to work." She placed her cup on its saucer and started to rise.

"Hold on."

"Yes?" She regarded him with raised brows.

"I'm cutting back on my responsibilities at Flying M Enterprises until after the wedding."

Hope sat down, hard. "Y-you are? Do you think that's necessary?"

"Absolutely necessary. I'll go in a day or two a week, but the wedding will be *my* top priority, too. Hey, I can't ask more of the rest of you than I'm willing to give myself, can I?"

Any answer to that eluded her.

Trace tossed down a sheaf of papers, leaned back in his chair and stifled a yawn. Hope, at the desk in the sunny yellow sitting room, looked up with a smile.

She'd been at the ranch for three days and had accomplished more than in the previous three weeks. Was that because of—or in spite of—Trace's distracting help?

He stretched out his long denim-covered legs and she was struck anew by the graceful power of his muscular body, the masculine beauty of his face. The blue of his chambray shirt intensified the blue of his eyes, and the long sleeves were rolled up to reveal powerful tanned forearms. No longer did he look like the sophisticated Trace Morgan, head of Flying M Enterprises, but like...like a cowboy, she thought, her gaze settling on his booted feet. Cowboys were somehow more attainable. . . .

"Let's go for a ride," he said abruptly.

"Oh, no, no." She shook her head vigorously. "I've got too much to do, but there's no reason you can't."

His laughter teased, his words coaxed. "It's not that much fun to ride alone. Besides, you deserve a break. I didn't bring you out here to work you to death."

He hadn't? With what he was paying her, it was the least she could do. "At the risk of disappointing you, I feel obliged to confess that I don't know how to ride."

"I'm a good teacher."

She just bet he was! "I'm afraid of horses," she said desperately. "Please, Trace—"

"Please, *Hope*." Suddenly he was no longer teasing. "It's a beautiful day and we've earned a treat. Besides, I'm paying you to please, and it will please me greatly to take you riding.''

He stood up and held out a hand, his gaze penetrating. He made her feel naked and vulnerable, and yet she was unable to keep herself from putting her hand in his. Instantly his long, strong fingers closed over hers and she was lost.

They rode their horses slowly around the lake, Trace in the lead on his big black while Hope clung to a saddle atop a pretty little palomino mare named Cream Puff. Trace had assured her that this was a perfect beginner's mount and he'd been right, Hope conceded, rocking to the gentle gait.

Trace himself had adjusted the stirrups and explained how to communicate with her mount using knees and reins and voice. At first overwhelmed, Hope soon relaxed and began to enjoy herself.

It was, as Trace had said, a beautiful sunny day. Puffy little clouds wisped across the blue sky, and not so much as a breath of wind stirred the water's blue surface.

Trace pulled up his mount beneath a cluster of oak trees, and Cream Puff obediently followed suit. Smiling, Hope leaned over the flaxen mane to pat the little mare's neck.

Trace was right—she'd needed a little fresh-air diversion after the rigors of dealing with vendors and arguing with tradespeople. That had to be why she felt so wonderful.

"How you doin', cowgirl?" Trace drawled.

"So far, so good." She looked at him lounging in the saddle, completely at his ease, and laughed ruefully. "I think I could learn to like this."

He nodded, stepping out of the saddle and dropping the reins on the ground. "That's great, but I don't want you to overdo it. You'll be sore tomorrow as it is."

"Really?" She watched him walk to the left side of the mare, then lift his arms and hold out his hands. After a moment's hesitation, she swung her right leg over the saddle horn, put her hands on his shoulders and slid off.

He caught her with his hands beneath her arms and lowered her to the ground, letting her body slide slowly down his. Light-headed from the intimate contact, she stepped quickly away from him.

"It's beautiful here," she said breathlessly, turning toward the lake.

"I knew you'd like it."

His voice, directly behind her, sent a delicious shiver skittering down her spine. "I do. Thank you for bringing me."

He laughed. "There's a lesson here."

"Where?" Without thinking, she swung around to look into his face, shadowed and somehow mysterious beneath the brim of his Stetson. "What lesson?"

"That maybe I know more about what's good for you than you do. That maybe you should try trusting me a little more."

She shifted uneasily, edging away from his overwhelming presence. "I trust you," she said, her voice faint. She added quickly, "So tell me, have you decided which hotel we should use for out-of-town guests? I was thinking—"

Rattling on nervously with wedding minutia, she led the way to a fallen oak tree, its branchy tip extending out into the water. She sat down while he braced one booted foot on the tree trunk.

"And the silver toasting goblets will be ready tomorrow," she continued. "Lillian was going to go to the jewelers and check the engraving—make sure the names are spelled correctly and so forth—but under the circumstances that's probably not a good idea."

"What circumstances?"

"Why—" She frowned at him. "Her daughter, of course. She's really quite distracted by the whole thing. I hate to lay anything else on her until it's over."

Slowly he straightened. "Until what's over? I have no idea what you're talking about."

Was it possible? Looking into his face, she saw that it was, and sighed. "I'm sorry, she said she'd speak to you about it. Her daughter—you know, the one who lives in Florida?—is in the hospital. The doctors seem optimistic, but you know how mothers— Trace! Where are you going?"

She was talking to his back. He'd spun around to yank up the horses' reins. All she could do was hurry after him. He put his hands at her waist and tossed her into her saddle, and she caught her breath in astonishment.

"My goodness," she exclaimed, "what's the matter? What did I say?"

He leaped into his own saddle and brought the big black swinging around beside the placid mare. "This is family business," he grated. Leaning forward, he caught the mare's bridle near the bit.

"Hang on to the saddle horn, Hope," he flung at her, and dug spurless heels into the black's sides.

By the time they reached the house, Hope clung to the saddle horn, stiff with fear. She'd made the mistake of looking at the ground hurtling along beneath her horse's hooves, and the sight had made her so dizzy she'd almost fallen off.

What in the world was the matter with Trace? He had no right to terrify her this way! She'd give him a piece of her mind, she decided, the minute she felt solid ground beneath her feet once more. But when he lifted her to down, his expression was so tight and forbidding that she said nothing, just watched him toss the reins to a stable hand and stride away.

Unhappy and confused, she climbed the stairs to her room. Their ride had begun so beautifully. If only she knew what she'd done to upset him.

She spent the rest of the afternoon alone, whittling away at the various lists of things to do, to buy, to decide. At five she called Celebrations and spoke to Mrs. Casen.

"Don't you worry, honey," the woman said cheerfully. "That Lisa's a real go-getter."

"Oh." Hope bit her lip. Was that supposed to make her feel better?

Maybe Mrs. Casen heard dejection in that single word, for she rushed on. "Not as good as you, of course—nobody's got your way, Hope. But Lisa's pitchin' in and at least now you know your business will still be standin' when you're ready to come back to it."

I'm ready now, Hope thought, hanging up. Couldn't Celebrations have suffered at least a little from her defection?

Cleaning up for dinner only reminded her of Trace's strange behavior earlier. He was sure to be in a bad mood, and if he'd run into Lillian, she'd probably be upset, as well as worried.

Family business, he'd said cuttingly. Apparently he'd been putting up with Hope only by gritting his teeth and forcing himself all this time. It was clear to her now that he considered her a busybody and a troublemaker.

He must love his sister very much to go through all that's involved in putting on a wedding, she thought as she descended the stairs. Was there a way out of this mess? She couldn't think of one, not without throwing the entire event into disarray.

At the foot of the stairs, she paused to draw a deep breath. At least Sabrina had left the house in a good mood this morning. Lifting her chin and pasting a smile on her face, Hope turned toward the dining room. She must play this out—she had no other choice.

She'd taken half a dozen steps when an agonized shriek froze her to the spot.

Running through the doorway to the dining room, Hope skidded to a halt. Sabrina stood behind a dining room chair, gripping the chair back so tightly that her knuckles were white. Her eyes burned with a blue fire that would have singed an ordinary man.

But no ordinary man faced her. Trace didn't even acknowledge her loss of control. "Be reasonable," he said to his sister. "I'm thinking of your own good."

Hope took a step back. "E-excuse me," she murmured. "I didn't mean to intrude on *family business*." She couldn't help a resentful glance at Trace.

"Stay!" Bree cried. "This concerns you, too."

"The hell it does," Trace shot back at her.

"It concerns Andy and he's not here to defend himself, is he!"

"He doesn't have to, when he's got you to do it for him."

"What—what's..." Hope glanced from one to the other, wondering what in the world had gotten into them. She swallowed hard. "Maybe I should go, Bree." She backed toward the door, feeling a coward's relief. She hated, loathed and despised shouting matches, and this one promised to be a lulu.

Trace threw up his hands in evident disgust. "It's too late now. You're already here."

"No," Bree shouted, "go. I couldn't stand it if you took his side."

"Sabrina!" Hurt, Hope stood her ground. "I can't imagine what would make you say a thing like that."

"I'm sorry, but you're always making excuses for him. Oh, I'm just so upset!" Bree covered her face with quaking hands that muffled her voice. "Tell her, Trace! Tell her what you said to me!"

"I said—" Trace turned his withering gaze on Hope. "It's time Romeo and Juliet signed a prenuptial agreement. I had no intention of insulting the guy—"

"Oh, really?" Bree cut in savagely. "Only every chance you get!"

"Sabrina, that's not true. I'm trying to look out for your best interests. I'm not proposing we take anything away from Andy, but I do think it's important to maintain your financial independence."

"I won't be financially independent until the day I turn twenty-five and get my hands on my trust fund. What will you do then, big brother? You won't be able to interfere in my life any further."

"I'll cross that bridge when I come to it."

"Can't you imagine any man would want me for myself?" Bree's voice was filled with anguish.

"You're missing the point, Sabrina. If this man is going to marry my sister—"

"If? *If*!" Her voice soared on the second word.

"That's right, if!" Trace rammed a hand through his hair in obvious agitation. "If he's going to marry my sister, it won't be for what he thinks he can get out of her."

Hope screwed up her courage to intervene at last. "This is about a prenuptial agreement?"

Bree swung around as if to confront a new enemy. "Yes! And I won't stand for it, not now, not ever!" She stomped to the doorway. "Lillian! I need you to help me pack!" She cast a vengeful glance at her brother. "I'm going to California."

"Damn it, Bree! You can't just—"

"I can! I'm of age and I can do any damned thing I want to do, including marry the man I love. Lillian!" She looked around wildly for the housekeeper, who had not appeared.

"Lillian's not coming," Trace said flatly.

"She is, too! Lillian's on my side. I happen to now she thinks you're a bully and a brute."

Hope winced, sure that Lillian had never said or ndicated any such thing. She glanced at Trace, recoiling from the censure in his expression.

"You mean," he said with silky enmity, "that Lillian talks to someone other than *Hope*?"

CHAPTER EIGHT

"HOPE?" Sabrina looked and sounded mystified "I didn't know Lillian talked to Hope."

"Neither did I," Trace said in the same chill tone, "until very recently. Apparently everybody confides in our little Friday's child, the wedding consultant."

Both turned to the innocent bystander herself who had had quite enough of this. "If they do," Hope said with spirit, "it's because I know how to listen—something it wouldn't hurt you to learn Trace Morgan!"

His eyes narrowed dangerously. "Touché."

Sabrina looked annoyed. "What are you two talking about? Where's Lillian? What do you have to do to get some *help* in this house? *Lillian*!"

"Lillian's on her way to Florida." Trace glanced at the heavy gold watch on his wrist. "She should be boarding a plane right about now."

"Florida!" It was almost a wail from Sabrina "But I need her! What's she going to Florida for?"

"Her daughter's having surgery." Trace sounded irritated by the inconvenience. "Everything's being done for her—I spoke to her doctor. But to quote our resident busybody, you know how mothers are."

"No," Sabrina shot back, "I don't. How would I?" She appealed to Hope. "See what Andy's getting? A woman without the slightest idea what *family* means."

Trace flinched and white lines of strain deepened in his lean cheeks. Hope was sure Sabrina hadn't noticed how she'd hurt him, for she'd already started for the door. "Please, Bree, wait—"

Sabrina whirled. "I'm going to California—for the weekend or forever, if Andy will let me stay."

Trace's jaw hardened. "Then take this with you," he said, offering the papers clutched in one fist. "Tell him it's my idea—hell, it *is* my idea. He can check with his dear cousin, if he needs confirmation."

"Never!"

"What will it hurt to bring it up?" Trace argued. "Maybe he'll surprise you. Maybe he'll surprise *me* and sign the damned thing. Find out, Sabrina. Find out before it's too late."

Trace took the few steps that separated them, picked up Bree's fisted hand, pried the fingers apart and inserted the prenuptial agreement. Her hand clenched it in a spasm that twisted the wrinkled sheets even more.

For a moment she stared at her brother as if the very sight of him made her sick. Then, with a tortured cry, she ran out of the room.

Hope didn't know which sibling needed comfort most. She looked after Sabrina, then at Trace. "About Lillian..."

He turned on her, his eyes glittering. "What about Lillian?"

"Just that...she would never, ever call you a bully or a brute."

His smile mocked her good intentions. "I know that, Hope. But she'd think it. Just like you and Sabrina think it."

"No, that's not true. Bree said a lot of things she didn't mean because she's angry and upset."

"Then go to her," he said, his voice flat and uncaring. "Perhaps she needs you. I don't."

And he turned and walked out of the room.

There was no chance of talking Sabrina out of the trip, none whatsoever. Hope tried, even after the guilty realization that she was trying for Trace's sake more than for Bree's or Andy's.

Bree kept up a running commentary of complaint while she called the airport, called Andy and left a largely incoherent message on his answering machine, and finally threw a few things into a bag. With Hope at her heels, Bree stormed down the stairway into the foyer.

Where Trace waited. "Sabrina—"

"Enough, Trace!" She sucked in a deep, quivering breath. "I'm going, and that's final!"

"When will you be back?"

"I told you, I don't know. Maybe I can talk Andy into eloping so we can put an end to this whole charade."

She blasted through the door. Hope turned to Trace. "It'll be all right. She didn't mean—"

His expression stopped her cold. He looked completely bereft, more shaken than she could ever imagine him being. She took a step toward him, her hand rising in a gesture of support. "Trace—"

He turned his back on her support and walked away from her for the second time in less than an hour.

What was she to do now? Hope stood in the shadowed foyer feeling helpless . . . and afraid. Not a sound could be heard in the enormous house. She might as well be alone.

Slowly she climbed the stairs and walked to her room—no, not *her* room, merely the room temporarily assigned to the wedding consultant. Only now there might be no wedding.

Giving in to impulse, she walked to the desk and dialed Andy's number. He answered on the second ring.

"Andy, it's Hope. Did you get Bree's message?"

"Not yet. I just walked through the door."

"I see." Hope bit her lip, trying to think of a way to say it. "I—we've had a . . . a blowup here and Bree's on her way to California."

He groaned. "Now what?"

"More of the same, I'm afraid. Andy, Trace wants you to sign a prenuptial agreement, and Bree—"

"Damn it, what's wrong with that guy? Every time he mentions the prenuptial agreement, Bree digs in her heels a little more. If it was up to me, I'd sign the damned thing and be done with it but—"

"Could I tell him that?"

A long silence, and then a brusque, "No, don't waste your breath. He'd never believe it anyway. Besides, it's none of his damned business."

Andy, for all his easygoing ways, could be stubborn in his own right, Hope knew. She sighed. "Okay, it's up to you. But there's something else. Bree threw the possibility of an elopement in his teeth again and the very word makes him crazy. For some reason, it seems to be his worst nightmare. Andy, you wouldn't do that, would you? I mean, I'm back here devoting months of my life and thousands of dollars of Morgan money to this simple little ol' Texas wedding. I'd like to be sure we'll have a bride and a groom when the time comes."

Silence.

She panicked. "Andy? Promise me you won't!'"

He made a strangled little sound that came clearly across the wire. "No, I won't," he said at last, his voice heavy, "*this* time. But if the pressure doesn't let up, I can't guarantee anything over the long haul."

With no desire to add to that pressure, Hope changed the subject, extracting the information that the job was going well, that he missed Bree something awful, that he hadn't had a decent tamale or taco since he left Texas.

The conversation concluded, Hope found the silence even more depressing. She wandered to the French doors leading to her private balcony and paused to gaze over the immaculate grounds. Spring had crept in with its soft green growth while she wasn't looking.

Whirling away, she leaned against the glass squares of the door. Procrastination would get her nowhere. She knew what she had to do. She was just, for some reason, reluctant to do it.

She had to leave.

She had to get away from Trace Morgan and the 'lying M and back where people were simple and ncomplicated, said what they meant and meant vhat they said. She'd stay if she could do any good ere, but obviously, she couldn't. He didn't want er interfering in family business, he'd made that erfectly clear. He was angry at her for knowing nore about Lillian's problems than he did, and he eemed to blame her for Sabrina's temper.

And who knew? Maybe he was right. Maybe vhat she thought was second nature to her, caring bout others, was actually intrusive. Maybe she, Iope Archer, was nothing more than what he ac-used her of being—a busybody.

Smarting beneath the doubts he'd planted, she Iragged out her suitcase and threw everything in a umble inside. She'd leave quietly, sparing him the ecessity of firing her. She had some pride, after ll....

Or did she? Standing in the foyer with her suitcase n her hand, she glanced toward the quiet interior f the big house.

What if, in spite of everything, he needed her nd she wasn't there? She was sure he hadn't been ntentionally cruel, to her or to Sabrina. He loved is sister, so perhaps it was only natural that he'd e suspicious of Andy's motives. And there must e a good reason for him to be as rabid on the ubject as he obviously was.

She looked at the front door with longing, but till she hesitated. She didn't want to risk his wrath et again. No matter what she said to him, no matter how much she longed to comfort him, he would seek ulterior motives.

She'd be a fool to try, and Hope Archer was nobody's fool.

Or hadn't been, up to now. Dropping her suitcase to the marble floor, she spun around and plunged into the interior of the dark, quiet house. Fool or not, she had to try.

She had to.

She finally found him in the two-story great room overlooking the lake and the swimming pool. He stood before the glass wall, a drink in his hand. He looked up at her entrance, no hint of surprise on his face.

"I've been expecting you," he said.

"Really?" She wrung her chilly hands together at her waist. Only a few soft lights were on, bathing the huge room in a kind of twilight duskiness. "I...I wanted to tell you I'm leaving now."

Slowly he straightened and his gaze hit her like a laser beam. "You're going into town?"

"Not exactly. I'm going home."

She could see him digesting that piece of information. Finally he said, "I see. You don't want to be in the house alone with me, obviously. Don't you think that's a lot of trouble to go to when you'll just have to come back on Monday?"

"But I'm not coming back Monday—I'm not coming back ever!" The words burst from her, and she heard the hurt and disappointment in her own voice and shivered.

After a long moment's silence, he said, "I expected you to be angry. I didn't expect you to try to get out of a contract."

"I'm not angry." It was the truth. "And as far as that contract goes, I don't think you really believe there's going to *be* a wedding—not the one we're planning, anyway."

Once more he pinned her with the laser beam of his gaze. "Do you?"

She'd agonized over that question. "I'd say at the moment the chances are about fifty-fifty."

She barely heard his softly uttered, "Damn! If they elope—"

"They won't," she assured him. "At least, not this time. But if you keep pushing Bree there's no telling what might happen." She had to make him listen, for his sake, for his sister's sake, she had to. She hurried across the great space separating them until she stood before him. "The more roadblocks you throw in their path, the more impatient and determined they become. It's human nature, for goodness' sake. Somehow it's almost like..." She bit her lip.

"Like what? Go on, say it all." His voice was harsh and unforgiving.

"Like there's some other reason driving you...like you know you're doing more harm than good but can't help yourself."

He exhaled sharply, and she thought yet again that she'd gone too far and managed to offend him beyond redemption.

"I'm sorry," she murmured, shoulders slumping. "You've made it perfectly clear that you don't like me interfering in family business—"

His hand fell heavily upon her shoulder and he stared at her with an intensity she felt all the way to her toes. Still holding her there, he leaned over and put his glass on an end table.

"Have you ever heard anyone mention... Rebecca?"

"No."

"I think it's time you did."

He led Hope to one of the many couches in the room and pressed her gently down, then sat beside her. She waited with calm acquiescence, sensing that he hadn't intended to mention that name and now must work out in his own mind what he wanted to say.

Rebecca—obviously a woman who meant a lot to him. Surely he was not a jilted lover. Hope caught her breath at the unlikely thought that Trace could be so desperately hurt by a woman. It wasn't possible, and yet...

Perhaps she should have run when she had the chance. Too late to think of that now, for he began to speak, his voice strong and controlled.

"Did you know Sabrina and I have—had an older sister named Rebecca?"

Great relief washed over Hope. "I had no idea. No one's ever mentioned her to me."

"I'd be surprised if they had. She's dead."

"I'm so sorry." Impulsively she touched his hand where it lay on his knee. He didn't pull away.

"Rebecca was beautiful and bright—a lot like Sabrina, as a matter of fact. Like all the Morgan women, she also had a temper."

Hope squeezed his hand. "Unlike the Morgan men?"

His grim little smile was quickly gone. "That's right. Morgan men are models of composure."

Turning his palm up, he curved his long fingers around her hand. "Rebecca eloped with a man who was after her money—and he got it, too, every last dime. Everyone in the family warned her, but would she listen? You'd be surprised how fast a fortune hunter can squander that fortune once he gets his hands on it. And when the money was gone, so was he. He left Rebecca for another woman."

"That's awful, Trace, but marriages break up all the time, even when money's not involved."

"Maybe so, but she never got over it. She was only twenty-seven when she died in an accident— or maybe it wasn't an accident, the authorities weren't too sure. It happened in Argentina, where she'd followed him hoping for a reconciliation."

"I'm so sorry," she said again, wanting to find words that would comfort him but falling back on clichés. "And you think Andy's like that? You couldn't be more wrong! Andy doesn't care about Sabrina's money. He loves her."

Trace lifted her hand and pressed it against his chest. His clear blue eyes looked into her pleading brown ones. "It's human nature to care about money," he said in a tone filled with regret. "What do you see when you look at me, Hope?"

"Why, I see—" She caught her breath, realizing that she saw a man about whom she'd come to care deeply, perhaps even...love. Not love! She couldn't fall in love with a man like Trace Morgan!

A wry smile teased the corner of his mouth. "Come on, Hope, confess. Do you see a man or the Morgan fortune?"

Before she could set him straight, he pulled her onto his lap and kissed her.

At the first brush of his lips on hers, her yearning heart overflowed. Sliding her arms around his neck, she snuggled closer, aware of his fingers sliding through her hair, of his muscular chest pressing against her, of his strong thighs beneath her.

But most of all, aware of the incredible sweetness of his kiss. Here was the man who could make all her dreams come true, fulfill all her vague yearnings.

And that man was the most unsuitable of all.

He broke the kiss to press his mouth to her throat. Before she knew what he was doing, he'd lifted her off his lap and laid her back onto the couch. Following her down, he claimed her lips again, at the same time sliding his hands down to fumble at the top buttons of her blouse.

"Sweet Hope," he murmured against her cheek. "Honest Hope. So loving and giving. You can't bring yourself to admit that even you have trouble getting past all that money."

She let out a little cry, part pain and part disillusionment. Pressing her hands against his shoulders, she pushed him away and scrambled off the couch. The thunder of her heart filled her ears, and her breath came in great gasps.

"I don't care anything at all about your money," she cried, "but I *do* care about you." *Too much*! Thank God she caught herself before adding that. She rushed on, "And I care for Sabrina and Andy, too. I'm sorry about Rebecca, but you can't make one sister pay for the mistakes of the other."

"You think that's what I've been doing?" He spoke calmly enough, but there was an implacable note in his voice.

"Isn't it?" She brushed a faintly trembling hand across her eyes. "Trace, I won't let you use me to prove Andy's a jerk, because he isn't. And I won't fall into bed with you for all the money in the world." *No matter that it's taken everything I've got to resist—and the money has nothing to do with it!*

"I see. Then perhaps we'd better call it a night." He stood up, his unwavering gaze chilling her to the bone. "I'll take your bags upstairs."

"Take them to my car!" Could that be her, shouting? She was about to lose it entirely.

For what seemed like forever, they stared into each other's eyes. Hope blinked first.

"Please, Trace—"

He made an impatient gesture. "You're not going anywhere tonight, but I am. I'll be back tomorrow, and we'll settle this then."

"But—"

"We'll settle this tomorrow."

He spun around and stalked out of the room. After a startled moment, she followed.

She came down to breakfast the next morning with her mind made up. It hadn't taken much soul-searching to conclude that she dared not face the emotional hazards of staying here. The only way to protect herself was to bow out of this job—and out of Trace Morgan's life.

His was a world far different from her own, a world she could not begin to understand. Too bad she'd lost her heart to him before she'd had a chance to defend it.

Taking a deep breath, she walked into the dining room to find him already seated at the table, a cup of coffee in one hand and a newspaper in the other. He gave her a cool glance.

"Good—" She swallowed hard and tried again. "Good morning."

He nodded. She walked to the sideboard and poured herself a cup of coffee with hands that trembled. Turning, she lifted her chin. "Trace, I—"

"Before you go on, I think you'll be relieved to hear that Lillian called this morning."

"Is her daughter all right?"

"She came through with flying colors. They've already done the biopsy and it's negative."

"Thank heaven." Weak with relief, Hope sank into a chair and placed her cup and saucer on the table. She dragged her reluctant gaze up to meet his. "I'm sorry you feel I meddled in your personal family business where Lillian's concerned. I never meant to, I swear."

"I know that. I knew it at the time."

"You did?" She frowned. "Then why were you so angry at me?"

He folded his paper and placed it beside his cup, leaning forward on his elbows. His beautiful long-lashed blue eyes narrowed thoughtfully. "I wasn't angry at you, Hope. I...I was angry at myself. I take care of my own. I should have known."

She heard the self-censure in his tone, the injured pride, and her carefully prepared defenses melted away. "She didn't want to bother you when you were already upset about Bree," she explained earnestly. "That's also why she hadn't asked for time off. She knew you'd give it to her if she did, but—"

"She shouldn't have to ask. I should have known—and offered."

"You're very hard on yourself," Hope murmured, realizing for the first time how true that was. She fought a rush of sympathy. "When will Lillian be coming back?"

"That depends."

"On what?"

"On whether you've gotten over your little snit of last night." He picked up his newspaper again but didn't open it, instead gazing at her in open challenge.

She reared back in her chair, astonished. Why would he say something like that to her, when they'd been communicating so well? "My little *what*?"

"You heard me," he said pleasantly. "If you insist on moving out, I'll be on that telephone so fast it'll make your head spin. I'll call Lillian home, then let Sabrina and Andy know what little faith you have in them—"

"I'm not the one lacking in faith!"

"It'll sure look that way if you break your promise, not to mention your contract to plan their wedding."

"Th-this is blackmail," she protested, her voice shaky. "I can't believe you'd stoop so low."

"Try me." His lips curled back over even white teeth in a triumphant smile. "I know what I want, which right off the top puts me one up on you. I'm also ready to use any means at my disposal to get it."

She felt as if she'd been flattened by a runaway steamroller. "But why?" she whispered. "Why are you doing this to me? I don't understand."

"No," he said calmly, "I don't suppose you do. Maybe it's better that way." Reaching beneath the table, he pressed a hidden buzzer to summon a maid.

His ruthlessness shocked and upset her, more so because she knew he'd been brutally honest about his failure to be sensitive to Lillian's needs. Hope turned away, determined not to let him see the sheen of moisture in her eyes. Not that he'd care, even if he knew he'd upset her. It wasn't as if he valued her good opinion, after all.

She'd do well to remember that in future dealings, she thought forlornly. She sighed. Once Bree and Andy were safely married, she'd never have to lay eyes on Trace Morgan again.

That thought should have made her happier than it did.

Hope sat at her desk, making notes in her planning book. Trace's sudden appearance in the doorway gave her quite a start.

She hadn't seen him since breakfast and it was now half past three. She offered him a dose of his own medicine, a cool glance she'd spent hours cultivating. "Yes?" she said, striving for insolence and achieving mere anxiety.

"Have you spoken to Sabrina today?"

"No. Why do you ask?" She'd considered calling California but decided to give the two lovebirds as much undisturbed time as possible.

"It occurs to me that she may have forgotten bout tomorrow."

"Tomorrow?" Hope felt a vague shaft of pprehension.

His mouth settled into a sardonic curve. "Po-ntial wedding gowns—remember now? We're oing to have a whole vanload at the front door omorrow at eleven. Sabrina's already arranged for substitute at school."

"Oh, Lord!" Hope stared at him, aghast. She'd ompletely forgotten. Had Sabrina? She reached or the telephone.

While she dialed, Trace strolled uninvited into he room and leaned a hip against one corner of er desk. To look at him, you'd never dream he'd ver had a cross word with anybody, Hope thought vith irritation.

"Hi, Bree? It's Hope." She swiveled around so he wouldn't have to look at Trace.

"Hope! I've been worried about you. Does this nean you survived the brother from hell?"

Hope laughed weakly. "So far. Uh...how's Andy?"

"Mmm." It wasn't a word, it was a purr of sat-sfaction. "I'm so glad I came."

Hope darted a guilty glance at Trace. "I'm happy ou're...enjoying yourselves. Uh, Bree, when are ou coming back? I hope you haven't forgotten that ve're going to have a houseful of wedding gowns ere tomorrow."

"Sure, I remember."

"Thank heavens." She gave Trace a thumbs-up ignal.

"I just don't care."

"What!"

"You heard me, Hope. I've already got the da
off so I'm going to spend as much of it as I ca:
with Andy. I've got a flight out of L.A. Monda
at six."

"But—but what am I supposed to do about al
those wedding gowns?"

"Narrow down the field," Bree suggested cheer
fully. "You know what I like—"

"I do not!"

"Yes, you do. Try on the ones you like, then hol
out your top choices for me to look over when
get back."

"You don't know what you're asking! You can'
expect me—"

A new voice came over the wire—Andy's. "D
it for me, cuz. It'll give me time to calm her dow
before I send her back to Texas." He added, sott
voce, "Believe me, I'll need every minute of it."

And Sabrina in the background, laughing, happy
teasing, "Calm me down? Calm me down! I'll sho
you how calm I am—" A series of unidentifiable
noises and the line went dead.

Wide-eyed, Hope looked at Trace. "She won'
be back until late Monday."

She saw relief on his face, quickly hidden, and
realized he hadn't been sure until that moment that
his sister would be coming back at all.

"And she wants you to screen the wedding
gowns," he guessed.

"That's right." Hope dug her nails into the desk
pad. "I don't feel right about doing it, though. It's
too big a responsibility. A wedding gown's a very
personal thing."

He grinned, a wide-open smile with nothing hidden and nothing missing. It dazzled and alarmed her, but most of all, it made her vulnerable to anything he might say or do.

What he said was, "Don't worry. I'll be there to help you."

What he did was pick up her hand off the desktop, raise it to his lips and kiss it.

Then he replaced it carefully on the blotter, turned and sauntered out of the room.

Leaving   behind   one   very   confused bridal consultant.

CHAPTER NINE

WEDDING gowns galore...

One heavy plastic bag after another passed through the front door at the Flying M that Monday, each on its own special padded wooden hanger and stuffed with tissue paper to protect the yards and yards of satin and silk, organza, taffeta, chiffon, beads and pearls, gossamer lace and heavy brocade, cathedral trains and ballerina-length hemlines, candlelight, alabaster, ivory and winter white—

Hope turned to Trace in a panic, managing to utter a single word. "Help!"

Trace had been standing back as if determined not to challenge her authority. Once sure of his welcome, he appeared more than willing to step into the breach.

"Carry all that stuff into the great room," he instructed. "The library can serve as a dressing room."

"Excellent!" The woman who'd introduced herself as Rose clapped her hands sharply and spoke to her two assistants. "Bring in the racks and the boxes of shoes and veils and accessories and put them—"

Still issuing orders, she herded the two down the hall.

Hope sighed. "What have we got ourselves into?" she wondered plaintively.

"If *you* don't know, we're in a lot of trouble," Trace retorted, but with an underlying good humor that brought a reluctant smile to her lips.

This was the charismatic Trace who enchanted her, not the hard and caustic stranger who'd turned on her vengefully, or even the sexy man who'd come close to seducing her. Following him into the great room, she reminded herself once again that she dared not let her guard slip when she was with him. No matter which of his many faces he chose to show her, one bitter fact remained. Any personal relationship between them would invariably lead to heartache—hers.

Rose turned with an unctuous smile. "Now, Ms. Morgan, allow me to show you what I've brought."

"I'm not Ms. Morgan, I'm Hope Archer, the wedding consultant. Ms. Morgan is...out of town."

"Good grief!" The woman's expression plainly added, *Then why have I dragged dozens of wedding gowns all the way out here?*

Trace intervened smoothly. "Ms. Archer will make the initial selection for Ms. Morgan's final approval. Since they're the same size, Ms. Archer will be trying on the gowns."

Rose heaved a sigh of relief. "In that case—" She clapped her hands smartly. "Let the games begin!"

"We call this model the Royal Princess, and it's perfect for the type of fairytale wedding you've described," Rose enthused. "You won't see many gowns like this, I can guarantee."

Hope stared at the gown, her brown eyes doubtful. It was all Trace could do to stifle a smile.

He didn't blame her dubious response in the slightest. The gown overwhelmed her slender form with masses of ruffles—organza tiers, Rose called them. More ruffles formed puffy sleeves, which stood up so stiffly they ticked Hope's chin when she turned her head.

"The bodice is of reembroidered lace with pearl accents," Rose explained with professional enthusiasm. "Isn't that heart-shaped mesh insert delightful? And the pearl-encrusted headpiece is the pièce de résistance!"

Hope rolled her eyes up as if to see this marvelous headcovering, which of course she couldn't. Just as well, Trace thought, looking at a veil so stiff and full that it created a halo effect around her head.

She didn't look like a princess, she looked like Little Bo Peep run amok. All she needed to complete the picture was a tall crook with a bow. It wasn't easy to keep from laughing but he managed, although his shoulders shook from the effort.

"Glorious, simply glorious." Rose stepped back to consider the effect, her head cocked. She turned to Trace. "What do *you* think, Mr. Morgan?"

"It . . . might be a bit much."

Rose shifted gears in a twinkling. "You're absolutely right. She has such a lovely figure that we should show it off, not hide it. Not to worry. We have plenty more where that came from."

She herded Hope into the library and closed the door, while Trace settled back to wait. When Hope reappeared, she was sheathed in a floor-length skintight silver-flecked off-the-shoulder number that revealed considerable cleavage. A long full satin train, banded with three inches of shiny silver, dragged along behind her, attached over her sassy little bottom by a huge white and silver bow. A puffy silver-speckled veil and elbow-length silver gloves completed the picture.

The absolutely hysterically funny picture.

Hope glared at him. "Don't laugh!" she ordered. "Don't you dare laugh, Trace Morgan!"

And then *she* laughed, her honey-brown eyes sparkling with amusement at her own predicament. The sophisticated dress might not be appropriate, but the slim elegance of her body did it justice and then some, Trace decided. He stared at the creamy rise of her breasts above the white and silver cloth, let his gaze slide slowly down to her tiny waist and the womanly flare of her hips.

Suddenly laughter was the last thing on his mind.

In a waiting mode once more, Trace reminded himself that when he looked at the next gown, he had to imagine it on his sister, not on Hope. Hope was nothing more than a living mannequin. She happened to be the right size, but she wasn't the bride.

Some day... What a beautiful bride she'd be for some lucky man. Lucky? He couldn't believe that word had even sprung into his mind. "Weddings" and "luck" in the same sentence represented a complete oxymoron, as far as he was concerned.

A rustling sound drew his attention and he looked around to find Hope standing in the doorway. And he stared....

She wore a simple satin gown, demure with its high neckline, dropped waist and long, pointed sleeves. A paisley design worked in pearls and subtly colored brilliants twined gracefully down the front the sleeves and around the sweeping hemline. A lacy crown, covered in the same pearls and brilliants perched atop an airy veil that swept the floor at he approach.

She gave him a tremulous smile, and he saw the shine of sentimental tears in her eyes. "This is the most beautiful thing I've ever seen," she whispered, smoothing her hands over the lustrous ma terial. "What do you think, Trace?"

"Beautiful," he agreed, looking full into her face.

She gave him a dazzling smile, then turned to Rose. "We'll put this one aside for Ms. Morgan to consider," she said happily.

Trace felt a slight pang, then smiled wryly. For Sabrina's consideration, of course. But he couldn't imagine she'd look as good in it as Hope did.

It took hours and hours, but at last six wedding gowns hung side by side on their own rack outside Sabrina's bedroom door. Three pairs of shoes and assorted crowns, headpieces and veils of every length and description were arranged nearby, blocking off one entire end of the broad hallway.

Rose had taken everything else away, to Hope's vast relief. Fluffing out the skirt of one of the gowns, she sighed.

"Tired?" Trace asked. "It couldn't be fun, climbing in and out of all those dresses."

"I'm tired, but it was a *lot* of fun, actually."

"Really?" He didn't sound convinced.

She looked pensively at the lacy confection in her hand. "I'll never own anything like this."

"A wedding gown? Come on. You'll get married."

"I certainly hope so." She dropped her hand, turning toward him with a smile. "I mean I'll never own anything this expensive or elegant. Not that I mind. When I do get married, I'll probably make my own wedding dress, and that will be special, too. But once in a while, it's fun to pretend."

He was frowning and she wondered what she'd said to irritate him this time. Although she found it almost impossible to anticipate his reactions, she understood her own with increasing ease. And the truth was, standing before him today in all these beautiful creations had almost broken her heart.

She wanted to be a bride, all right—this man's bride. Unfortunately, he saw her only as the hired help, stand-in for his sister, a worker bee hired to plan the perfect wedding. He wasn't interested in her silly little fantasies.

She gave him her most brilliant smile. "I hope Bree likes what we've chosen," she said, her tone businesslike once more.

"She will."

"You sound awfully sure of yourself."

He shrugged. "I'm not worried about the gown, I'm worried about the bride. If Sabrina and your cousin decide to jump the gun—"

"They won't," Hope interrupted firmly. "They know what's going into this, all the time and money and hard work. They'd never let everyone down that way."

"Oh, no?" He raised his brows. "You don't know Sabrina."

"I think I know her better than you know Andy," she retorted.

"Don't be too sure. I hear that men in love do strange things for their women. If Andy really care for her—"

"He does!"

"Then I rest my case."

Hope stared after his retreating form. Could he be right? So far Andy had stood firm in the face of Bree's entreaties, but could he continue to do so? What if she gave him an ultimatum?

She seemed so insecure that she just might. What if she demanded Andy prove his love by marrying her immediately? What if she decided it was now or never?

No! Hope yanked such disloyal thoughts up short. Trace had planted all these suspicions. She mustn't let him shake her faith. She *wouldn't*.

Sabrina joined them for breakfast Tuesday morning, a subdued and quiet Sabrina.

She's tired, Hope thought, listening to her monosyllabic responses. Had she had a good flight? *Yes*. Was the weather pleasant in California? *Yes*. Did she have a chance to do any shopping for her trousseau? *No*.

Hope reached for another croissant. "I can't wait to show you the gowns we held back," she said cheerfully, determined to arouse a response. "I'm sorry you missed Rose and her traveling troupe. She really brought some humdingers." She glanced at Trace and found him looking at his sister through narrow eyes. "Didn't she, Trace?" she added quickly.

"Yeah," he said easily. "I was especially fond of the one that made you look like Little Bo Peep. We could have rented a flock of sheep for the day and let Sabrina wade through 'em to get to the altar."

Sabrina looked up from her plate, where she'd been shoving around a chunk of orange. "Sounds good," she said vaguely. She laid down her fork and rose, dropping her napkin on the table. "I'm sorry, I've got to get to school. We'll choose the gown tonight."

Trace waited until she left the room before looking at Hope with an accusation in his eyes. Hope looked back with anxiety in her heart.

"Something's wrong," he said flatly.

"Now, we don't know that," she tried to soothe his fears. "She's probably just miserable because she had to leave Andy and come back home."

"That's what worries me. If she gets miserable enough, she may decide *not* to leave him next time."

"Well, it's your own fault, Trace." Hope jumped to her feet, astonished at herself for lighting into him this way. But she'd had enough. She just had to say what was on her mind. "You're the one who insisted on turning a simple little wedding into the extravaganza of the century. If you'd been reasonable, we wouldn't be going through all this because they'd be married already!"

He answered her with cold calculation. "What makes you think I'd prefer to have them married already? I'd walk through fire to stop this marriage. Every day I stall, she's a day closer to realizing what he's really after."

The bottom fell out of Hope's world and she sat down hard. Trace wasn't reconciled to this marriage and never would be. Here she was, planning a dream wedding for a bride who didn't want it, being paid for by a man who considered it the lesser of two evils.

Apparently it was nobody's dream but hers. She watched Trace stand up and walk out of the dining room, taking her now-shattered illusions with him.

Somebody had to keep life at the Morgan ranch on an even keel, and Hope was forced to conclude that the job was hers by default. She was, as Trace had told her so bluntly, being paid to please. If grit and determination could snatch success from the jaws of failure, she would not stint in her efforts.

Lillian's return at the end of the week helped. Sabrina welcomed the housekeeper with open arms. When Lillian sought Hope out later to thank her for intervening with Trace, Hope couldn't help asking about Lillian's unique position in the Morgan household.

Lillian responded with a searching glance. "I do think it's time we had a little talk," she said grimly. "I'll get us a pot of tea and meet you in the solarium in five minutes. No one will disturb us there."

Heart in her throat, Hope waited as directed, then accepted a cup of tea, turned down a cookie and drew a deep breath. "Tell me about the Morgan family," she asked with quiet determination.

Lillian sighed. "It's a wonder Trace and Sabrina are as well-adjusted as they are." She rolled her eyes for emphasis. "Their parents had a miserable marriage. He was a workaholic and she was flighty and

ompletely lacking in maternal instinct. I'm sorry
that sounds harsh but it's true.''

Thinking of the three Morgan children raised in
uch an uncaring environment, Hope swallowed
ard. ''Poor little things,'' she murmured.

Lillian nodded. ''Believe me, I never set out to
ake their mother's place. I had a family of my own
nd besides, it just wasn't right. But I was always
round and she was always someplace else—Paris,
ondon, Rome. It wasn't so much that she didn't
are, I've always thought. She was just an ex-
emely selfish woman.''

''And when she was gone, Trace and Bree and
ebecca turned to you for comfort.'' Understand-
ble, yet so very sad.

Lillian picked up a cookie, put it back on the
late absently. ''Not Rebecca so much. She was
lder, and a lot more like her mother than Trace
ould care to admit. It almost killed him when they
ied within six months of each other.''

''He . . . he told me a little about Rebecca.''

''I'm surprised.'' Lillian gave Hope a probing
ance. ''He tried so hard with Becky, and felt his
ilure so completely. I don't know what he ex-
cted, really. He was only seventeen and Bree eight
hen Becky died. That same year his parents di-
rced and then his mother was lost with a number
f her socialite friends in the crash of a private
ane.''

All that tragedy, all that loss. No wonder Trace
ld himself aloof so much of the time.

Lillian leaned forward to pat Hope's knee.
Trace was mad at you, wasn't he.'' It was not
ally a question.

Hope grimaced. "Which time?" she aske[d] lightly. "He spends most of his time mad at me, i[t] seems."

The housekeeper sighed. "Don't give up on him[,] hon. There is no finer, more loyal man on the fac[e] of this earth than Trace Morgan."

"I know that." Hope looked away, afraid Lillia[n] would see too much in her eyes. "I think now I ca[n] understand why he's so worried about Sabrina."

"Not . . . entirely."

"Oh, Lord, what else?"

Lillian toyed with her teacup. "Bree's a darlin[g] and I love her dearly but she's always been [so] little . . . let's be nice and call it immature."

"Well, yes, maybe a little, but . . ." Hope frowned[.] "Is there something I don't know?"

"You tell me. Do you know about her othe[r] engagements?"

"She's been engaged to be *married*? Wha[t] happened?"

"To quote you—which time? She's pretty, she'[s] rich and she's always attracted the fellas." Lillian['s] laugh sounded indulgent. "She always saw the ligh[t] herself and broke it off, except once."

"What happened?"

"It was a boy very much like Andy, at least o[n] the surface. He came from a respectable, if n[ot] wealthy, family. He'd had to scratch for what h[e] had and from the first, Trace was convinced h[e] wasn't on the level."

Hope's mouth went dry. "What did Trace do?"

"Bluntly stated, Trace bought him off. Sat dow[n] and wrote him a check and that was that."

Hope closed her eyes, feeling a bit of what Bree must have felt. "It's a wonder she ever forgave him," she said faintly.

"We weren't sure she ever would, but finally she came around...at least on the surface. Deep down, I doubt she'll ever completely trust her brother again. Love him, yes. Trust him—" Lillian shook her head sorrowfully.

It was all coming much clearer to Hope now—Trace's doubts were about Bree, as well as Andy. "Trace tried to buy Andy off, too," she said slowly, "but it didn't work. Andy absolutely adores Bree. He'd never hurt her. As for her money, it's a curse to him, not a blessing."

"Yes, I believe that." Lillian spoke emphatically. "Nobody's told me but I'll bet dollars to doughnuts Bree won't let him sign that prenuptial agreement. Am I right?"

Hope nodded. "I gather they've had awful fights about it. He understands her point—that she's standing on principle—but since he'd never touch a penny anyway, he'd sure like to get Trace off his back by signing." She laughed wryly. "Maybe on their tenth anniversary—"

"Don't count on it," Lillian said tartly. Then her expression softened. "Hope, you've been a wonderful influence around here." She gave a teasing smile. "You weren't by any chance born on a Friday, were you?"

Hope blinked in surprise. "How did you guess? Is it so obvious?"

"Friday's child is loving and giving," Lillian quoted. "That's you in a nutshell, honey—loving and giving."

The praise brought a flush of embarrasse pleasure to Hope's cheeks. "That's very nice of you Lillian, but I wish I could do more," she sai honestly. "The problem is, I really can see every body's side. Andy just wants to get married, Bre seems to be afraid he'll get tired of the hassle an leave her standing at the altar. Then there' Trace...." She realized she probably had a sapp expression on her face and wiped it away. "Trac is going to have to learn to trust those he love enough to let them find their own way or he's goin to end up—" She stopped, appalled at the di rection her thoughts had taken her.

"Say it," Lillian urged. "You're among friends.'

"Trace is going to end up exactly where he i now," Hope whispered, "a very rich, very...lonel man. And that would be such a horrible waste."

She shoved her teacup onto the table, leaped t her feet and ran out of the solarium.

Lillian sat there quietly for several minutes staring out over the swimming pool. Then she rose gathered up the tea things, carried them into th kitchen and went in search of Trace.

Trace looked up impatiently from the files sprea open across his desk. Although he only went int his corporate headquarters once or twice a weel now, that didn't mean he was relieved of responsi bility as head of the giant firm. It simply meant h conducted more and more business from this offic on the first floor of the ranch house.

To his surprise, he found he enjoyed workin at home.

Usually. He skewered Lillian with an unfriendly gaze. "Yes?"

She looked pointedly at the cluttered desk. "I botherin' you, Trace?"

He shrugged. He didn't like her stern expression or the pugnacious lift of her shoulders. "You, Lillian? Never." He tossed his pen atop the mess and leaned back. "What can I do for you?"

"You can accept my resignation." Marching to the desk, she dropped a single sheet of paper in front of him. "The wedding's June 15. This takes effect June 16."

For a moment Trace sat in stunned silence, then he leaped to his feet with an incredulous roar. "The hell it does!" He grabbed up the sheet of paper and ripped it into shreds.

Lillian didn't shrink before his fury. "I can always write another one," she said. "Trace, it's for the best. I'm going to move to Florida to be near my daughter and the grandkids. I've wanted to for years. What's so bad about that?"

He thrust a hand through his hair. "I don't think this place can run without you. My God, Lillian, you've been here for thirty years—my entire lifetime. You've been like a moth—" He snapped his mouth closed on the word. She'd been a mother to him and to Sabrina, but she *wasn't* their mother, and even if she were, they were adults now.

Her expression softened and she reached out to stroke his taut cheek. "You can say it, Trace— mother. I'm mighty proud to have helped you and your sister through the . . . difficulties of your early years. But I'm not your mother. If I were, though,

I'd tell you the same thing—that it's time for all of us to get on with our lives, you included.''

"What the hell is that supposed to mean?'' He couldn't believe she was serious. To lose his sister and the woman who'd virtually raised him, both within the course of twenty-four hours—

It was too damned much. He wouldn't stand for it.

Lillian sighed. "Trace, honey, let go. Sabrina has found her happiness, and you'd do well to get out of her way and let her have it. Mine's in Florida and I'm goin' after it. None of which means we don't love you, 'cause we do.''

"It sure as hell doesn't sound like it,'' he snarled.

"You're surrounded by love and you don't even know it,'' Lillian said sadly. "Maybe you'll never know. For your sake, I hope...'' She gave him a look brimming with sympathy. "Never mind. I know you don't cotton to lectures and you don't like advice, so I won't give you any more. Even when you were a little boy, you liked to figure out your own answers. I'll leave you to it and go tell Sabrina.''

"You do that,'' he said harshly. He turned to the window, staring at the broad front lawn with its white fences and graveled driveways.

It seemed as if all the women in this house had lost their minds at the same time—all except Hope of course. And they were all blaming him. His crime? Trying to do what was best for those he loved.

To hell with that. Caring only made him vulnerable. He didn't like being vulnerable.

But he did like having an ace in the hole....

* * *

Bree chose the beautiful gown of Hope's dreams, and the rejects were sent back to the bridal salon. Hanging the winner in its own special closet in a guest room, Hope wondered if she'd exerted undue pressure in its selection.

The truth of the matter was, Bree didn't much seem to care. Ever since the trip to California, she'd been subdued, even a bit secretive. Nothing seemed to get a rise out of her, not even Lillian's bombshell.

Hope had felt guilty about that, too. She'd gone to Lillian and asked hesitantly if their conversation had had anything to do with this sudden resignation. The housekeeper assured her it hadn't. Hope wasn't entirely convinced.

It seemed to her that they were all turning their backs on Trace at the same time. *He doesn't deserve that kind of treatment*, she thought, incensed in his behalf. She felt so bad that she went out of her way for him even more.

Not that he seemed in need of comfort. As the days passed into weeks, he became, if anything, even more charming. Not a critical word passed his lips, so far as she could tell, not about the wedding or Bree or Andy or anyone or anything. Where Bree reminded Hope of a time bomb waiting to explode, Trace reminded her of someone who'd already read the last page of the book and knew exactly how everything was going to turn out.

As June 15 drew inexorably nearer, the pace of wedding preparations accelerated. Gifts flowed into the house in a never-ending stream of silver and crystal and china. There were parties for the bride-to-be, and for the wedding couple when Andy could make it back for a weekend.

Sabrina was only going through the motions
Hope feared. And watching her brother, always
watching her brother...

What was she expecting? Finally, the day after
the wedding rehearsal, Hope had to ask.

"He's up to something," Sabrina said, sounding
paranoid. "He'd never give up, not as long as
there's breath in his body. I don't know what he's
planning but it's something—something horrible.
I almost wish it would happen so we could get it
over with."

"But you're being married in two days, Sabrina,"
Hope soothed. "What could he possibly do now,
even if he wanted to—which I don't for a minute
admit he does."

"I don't know," Bree confessed, then leaned
forward to give Hope a sudden unexpected hug.
"If I don't get another chance to tell you, I want
you to know how much I appreciate everything
you've tried to do for us. Without you, I don't think
I'd have made it this far."

Hope returned the hug. "Is something else bother-
ering you?"

Bree's laughter sounded brittle and insincere. "Of
course not. Gotta run—Andy's waiting. Don't
worry about me, Hope. One way or another, I'm
finally going to get everything I've ever wanted."

Alone, Hope bit her lip, wondering what she
should do. At the risk of rocking the boat at the
last minute, perhaps she should go to Trace and tell
him—what? That his sister still didn't trust him?
He knew that.

Her uneasiness growing, she decided to go on
back for one last look at the enormous tents already

ected over the tennis courts. Canopies sur-
ounded the swimming pool, and gardeners had
ent weeks digging and planting, carting plants and
aterials in and out, arranging the enormous
arble urns containing trees and shrubbery and
owers.

Tomorrow—Friday, the day before the
edding—the final touches would be applied to a
ene already transformed into a fairyland. A
illion and one last-minute details would demand
tention. Saturday was the day, the day no one
cept Hope had apparently ever really thought
uld come.

Then on Sunday, Cinderella's coach would
come a pumpkin once more when Hope returned
her own little house and her own little business
d her own little life. At least she'd go secure in
e knowledge that she'd done the best possible job
e could under the circumstances.

She'd take something else with her, too—the sure
d certain knowledge that she had left her love
hind her.

CHAPTER TEN

By TEN o'clock Thursday night, Hope was s
nervous she simply couldn't concentrate on her list
any longer. Letting herself out of the room an
closing the door gently behind her, she walked dow
the broad hallway and paused at the head of th
sweeping staircase.

The house was quiet, perhaps too quiet after th
cacophony of the last several days. If she close
her eyes, she could almost remember what life wa
like in more peaceful days.

She might as well face facts—it was going to ge
worse before it got better. Steeling herself for an
chance encounter with Trace, she hurried to th
kitchen and peeked inside.

It was empty, every pot and pan in its place an
every surface gleaming. Hope sighed, realizing she
expected to encounter Lillian. Apparently th
housekeeper had retired for the night. Hop
wouldn't dream of disturbing her.

But she felt so restless and alone. She wandere
aimlessly into the great room, now piled high wi
items that would be needed Saturday; tables, chai
lighting equipment—who knew what all this stu
was? Remembering the engagement party and t
way she'd transformed this elegant room into
barn, Hope smiled.

Trace hadn't minded at all. In fact, he'd prov
himself to be a man of rare flexibility. He had on

he blind spot that she could see—his proprietary
titude toward those he loved.

Those lucky few he loved...

She could see through the glass wall that the
nderwater lights had been left on in the swimming
ool. The water glowed with an unearthly incan-
scence that drew her outside. Leaning against the
rought-iron railing on the deck, she stared down
to the shimmering depths.

She had never dreamed such a life-style as this
isted. That Sabrina was so willing to give it up
oke volumes about her loving commitment to her
ncé.

Hope understood, for when she herself left, it
uldn't be the luxury she would miss here, it was
e boss man of the Flying M himself, Trace
organ—

Arms slipped around her in a snug caress. She
sped and recoiled, inadvertently thrusting herself
ther into an embrace she hadn't anticipated. She
ew who held her by the racing of her pulse, even
fore Trace spoke in her ear.

"Looks as if everything's under control."

Except my heart... "Y-yes. I hope I'll be able
say the same this time Saturday."

"You will. I have complete faith in you."

He curled his body around hers, his chest pressing
ainst her shoulder blades and his arms beneath
breasts. Too late she realized she should have
otested long before now.

"Trace—" she began on a warning note.

He nuzzled her ear, making her shiver with
asure. "I know," he said. "You've made it clear
u prefer a strictly professional relationship. It's
t that we've been through so much together.

You'll be leaving soon and I suddenly realized I've gotten used to having you around. I...I'm going to miss you, Hope.''

She bit back a groan. "I'll miss you, too—and Bree and Lillian and everyone else.''

He curved his hands over her hips, fingers splayed. "I hope you mean that. When I saw you from my window, it occurred to me that...neither of us should be alone tonight.''

She knew exactly what he was saying to her in that low, caressing tone. *This is your last chance.* Perhaps her last chance to ever know love...

She stood very still, telling herself she must be strong. For as certainly as she knew the sun would rise tomorrow, she also realized that if she ever gave in to her feelings for him, she would never again be a whole person in her own right.

A little of Trace Morgan would never be enough. And that's all he was offering her, or ever would.

Almost as if she were in a trance, she put her hands over his and unwrapped his arms from around her. With one quick, frightened step, she was free to face him.

He looked at her with a possessiveness that made her shiver, his slight smile dangerously compelling. "You feel the same way I do," he said, as if there could be no doubt. "Don't bother to deny it, Hope. You'll come with me now because you want to. No more games...just you and me. Don't you think it's time we were honest about our feelings?''

Honest? she thought wildly. Surely he didn't want her to be honest about how hopelessly she adored him. If she loved him less, she probably would have fallen into his bed long before now. As it was, she knew instinctively that physical intimacy would

way her final mooring and leave her adrift with
nothing to sustain her afterward.

And there would be an afterward, for he had
given no hint of any deeper feeling.

"I'm sorry," she whispered, dizzy from the effort
to resist what he offered. "I want to be with you—
more than you'll ever know. But not this way. Not
because you're lonely, or because someone else has
disappointed you. I couldn't survive that."

He didn't reply, simply offered his hand in a
gesture that proved irresistible to her. As one hyp-
notized, she put her trembling hand in his....

With a low, triumphant exclamation, he drew her
into his arms and kissed her. The touch of his lips
sent wildfire roaring through her veins. His hands
stroking her back made her shudder with longing.

And still he kissed her, until she tingled from head
to toes with a desire she could not begin to conceal.
Only then did he lift his face to look at her. "I'll
take care of you, Hope," he murmured. "Come
with me—it's what you want. Follow your
feelings...."

"I can't," she cried. "If you knew how I really
feel, you wouldn't want me to."

She felt his muscles tense where their bodies
touched. He frowned at her, still locked in his arms.

"What's that supposed to mean?" He allowed
just the slightest loosening of his embrace, looking
at her with hooded eyes.

She stared back with her heart in her throat.
Dared she gamble with the truth? Why not? She
had nothing to lose because nothing had ever been
hers, not where he was concerned.

Certainly not his heart.

"It means—" She sucked in a deep breath and turned her head aside, unable to look at him any longer. "I'm in love with you, Trace. Through no fault of your own—heaven knows, you never encouraged me to believe you could care for me beyond casual friendship—no, even friendship's too strong a word. You hired me to do a job and you're paying me for that, not for friendship or . . . or anything else."

This was horrible; this was unreal. She covered her eyes with quaking hands and stepped out of his suddenly slack hold. She had to force herself to continue in a voice that threatened to break. "But that's all you're paying me for, to plan a wedding. Loving you was my own idea—well, not exactly an idea—more something I couldn't help. Oh, I'm such a fool! Maybe if you didn't have all that damned money—but you do and there's nothing to be done about that."

She gritted her teeth at the unfairness of it all. Opening her eyes, she found him staring at her as if she'd entirely lost her mind. Humiliated, she gave a weak little laugh. "You wanted honest," she said, "and you got honest. I'll bet you're sorry you asked."

He stood there for a moment, stock-still. Then, with a muffled exclamation, he turned and walked quickly away, his athletic shoes soundless on the wood and tile deck.

Choking back a sob, she slumped against the pool railing. If she wasn't going to sleep with him, she probably shouldn't be surprised he didn't care enough to stay and hear her silly little declaration of love.

* * *

Hope pressed her cheek against Sabrina's bedroom door and patted the wooden surface with the flat of one hand. "Bree," she called softly, "are you there?"

No answer. Hope sighed. It was a few minutes past eight on Friday, the day before the wedding, and there'd been no sign of the bride-to-be as yet. "Sabrina, answer me," she all but begged.

Again her hand came down on the door, unexpectedly causing it to swing open a couple of inches. Frowning, Hope leaned closer to the opening and called again.

Nothing. With a final hard rap of her knuckles, she shoved the door wide and walked inside.

"Sorry, Bree," she said briskly, "but we don't have time to lollygag in bed on the day before the day—"

She stopped short. Bree wasn't here, that much was instantly apparent. Her lovely aqua-and-white bedroom was turned topsy-turvy, clothing and cosmetics and books and papers and magazines and Heaven only knew what else strewn from one end to the other.

But no Bree. Hope felt the first stirrings of panic. Perhaps Bree had an early appointment; perhaps she'd already gone out. Perhaps—

And then Hope saw it—the note, taped on the dressing table mirror, with her name in big block letters. For a minute or two she simply stared at it, trying to fight back a sick feeling of impending doom.

It wasn't bad news; it couldn't be bad news! Hope yanked the heavy sheet of paper free and opened the single fold with trembling hands. It took a few seconds to focus her frightened gaze on the small precise printing.

Hope, I'm sorry but I have no choice. I only came back the other time because Andy asked me to give it one more try. He promised that if it didn't work, he'd go along with what I've wanted all along—to elope.

It's obvious to me now that Trace will never change his attitude so I'm doing the only thing I can do. By the time you get this note, Andy and I will be on our way to Las Vegas. Please try to understand. I don't care about the big wedding or the stupid gifts or the fancy gown—I never did. All I want is Andy, and now I'm going to have him, always. You can't know what a relief this is to me!

As for the wedding, I hope everyone will just have a big party tomorrow and drink a toast to us. Believe me, it's better this way. All my love,

Sabrina

P.S. I hope you don't mind telling Trace.

Hope felt as if the floor had been cut from beneath her feet. She sat down hard on the cedar chest at the foot of the bed, clutching the sheet of paper to her chest. She understood; of course she understood how beleaguered Sabrina must have felt to take such dire action.

But Trace wouldn't. Not in a million years. He'd never forgive Andy, or accept him. That was completely out of the question now.

And Trace would never forgive Hope, either, for she'd all but guaranteed her cousin wouldn't do anything so rash as elope. Oh, if only—

But she had no time for might-have-beens. It was
r duty to break the bad news to Trace. True, she'd
her have her fingernails pulled out one at a time
an face him, but no such easy way out presented
elf.

With her heart in her throat, she crept down the
irs and through the hustle and bustle of wedding
rkers. She'd never felt such an alien in this house,
t even the first time she'd entered.

She didn't want to be the one to tell him. After
at had happened between them last night, he
uld hate her...if he didn't already.

She found him in his office, a room she'd never
tered. At his muttered "Come in," she slowly
shed the door open and slipped inside, her head
ooping beneath the load of guilt she carried.

"Good morning," he said coolly. He laid the
per in his hand on top of the pile before him on
e desk blotter. "Sleep well, I presume?"

She felt a spark of rebellious spirit but tamped
down. She'd hardly slept at all, thanks to him,
t didn't feel she was in any position to say so.
Vell enough." She swallowed hard. "Trace,
re's something I have to..."

When she didn't go on, he raised his brow and
fered a calm, "Yes?"

He obviously wasn't going to make this any
sier. She dug her nails into her palms, managing
crumple the note in the process. "I...I just came
om Sabrina's room and—"

Again he said, "Yes?"

"Sh-she's not—I mean, she's...the door—and
ound a note—oh, Trace, I can't tell you how
ry—" Trembling to a halt, she dropped the piece
paper on his desk. Without waiting for him to

pick it up, she hurried on. "I know this will be
shock—it was to me, too. I have no idea wh
caused her to take such drastic action so close
her wedding day. But—"

He waved her quiet, picked up the note and beg
to read. She stood the silence as long as she cou
and then launched into another defense.

"I know you have no reason to believe anythi
I say at this point, but they're going to be happ
It's a shame about the wedding and the reception
all that time and effort, not to mention money
but that was never so much for them as it was f
you. And even me, I guess. Bree knew this was
big opportunity for Celebrations."

He finished reading and looked up at her. H
expression remained a complete blank, which scar
her, but at least he hadn't lost that famous Morg
temper.

She screwed up her courage to continue. "I kno
this looks bad but I'm still positive that Andy is
after Sabrina's money," she said bravely. "He tru
isn't, Trace."

"I know."

She blinked twice. "W-what did you say?"

"I said . . ." He turned the full force of brillia
blue eyes upon her. "I know."

Hope stumbled back a step and slumped into
leather chair. "B-but *how*? How do you sudden
know, when I've tried for months to convin
you?"

"I know," he said softly, "because of this." H
lifted a document from the pile before him an
shoved it across the desk toward her.

eaning forward, she read, *Prenuptial agree-
nt, entered into this twelfth day of June by
drew Lloyd Archer.*

'Oh, my God!'' She sank back in her chair, her
s wide. ''Where? How?''

race rose. ''It was delivered a few minutes ago
messenger, along with a note from Andy. Seems
've been right all along—it was Sabrina who
s against him signing. He did this without her
wledge, and according to his note, there'll be
l to pay when she finds out.'' His sudden grin
s a ray of sunshine through the gray clouds of
day. ''Smart guy, your cousin. Say he's not
ng to tell her until *after* they're married. But tell
he will, because he loves her, and secrets have
vay of coming back to haunt you—his words,
mine.''

stunned by this turn of events, Hope felt tears
relief gather behind prickly eyelids. But that was
nothing to what she felt when Trace slowly, de-
rately ripped the prenuptial agreement into
eds.

She half-rose from her chair. ''What are you
ng? I thought that's what you wanted!''

He gave her a gently admonishing look. ''What
anted was to be sure he loves her—that she loves
. That's why I waited up for Sabrina last night.''

So Bree had bolted because of something Trace
l to her. The final mystery solved. ''I'm almost
aid to ask what happened,'' Hope whispered.

'I offered to release her trust fund immediately
he'd drop the guy,'' he said bluntly, ''or failing
t, just live with him instead of getting married.''
lips twisted in a wry grimace. ''She told me in
uncertain terms what I could do with that trust

fund, and believe me, she didn't paint a pre
picture.''

Light-headed with relief, Hope shocked hers
by giggling. He had played his final card, and
had failed. Sabrina and Andy had apparently w
Trace over by doing the very thing he'd m
feared—but doing it in the right way.

Her relief was short-lived, for in the n
heartbeat she realized that her work here was do
now. She'd move out immediately, of course. S
had no choice, although she'd probably be luc
if she saw Trace once a year from now on. Whi
reminded her of their final problem—

''My God,'' she cried, jumping up. ''We hav
wedding of epic proportions planned for tomorr
afternoon and no bride or groom. What are
going to do, Trace?'' She wrung her hands, thinki
aloud. ''Of course, there'll be no charge for
services but the caterers—''

He came around the desk toward her but she k
talking. ''The florists, the tents, the lights a
everything else—so many people. What are
going to do?'' She reached for him, her har
crushing the lapels of his red silk shirt. ''Tra
speak to me! *What are we going to do*?''

''Hope Archer,'' he said with absolute co
viction, ''there's only one thing *to* do....''

Saturday, June fifteenth, arrived in a burst
golden glory. With the ceremony set for three-thi
guests began to arrive much earlier to stroll throu
the fabulous Flying M gardens and admire
fairytale setting for what promised to be the soc
event of the season. Something special was in

r, some magic that everyone seemed to feel and
are.

Bree's godfather, the judge, arrived and took his
osition. The orchestra switched from show tunes
 a joyous Mendelssohn. All eyes turned to watch
e wedding party march down a lovely aisle created
 fresh floral garlands ending at the flower-
decked archway, which created a lacy bower for
e ceremony.

When everyone was in place, the bride appeared,
earing a gown of extraordinary beauty and
vathed in a veil of net illusion. Carrying a bouquet
 white roses and orchids set off by trailing ivy,
e floated down the aisle as if happiness had truly
ven her feet wings. Beneath the canopy of flowers,
e turned—

And Trace Morgan strode forward, eliciting a
sp from the enormous assemblage of guests. With
 smile of infinite tenderness for his bride, he
ached out and lifted her veil himself. The airy net
ll gracefully over her shoulders and floated out
hind her.

With an abiding happiness that she knew would
ver leave her, Hope looked into the face of love.
e judge began to speak, and each word seemed
 her as fresh and new and filled with promise as
 it had never been heard before today.

And all because Trace loved her. He'd told her
 for the first time yesterday, in his office.

"When I thought of you leaving, I knew I
uldn't let that happen," he'd said, his voice strong
th emotion. "About halfway through planning
is wedding, it stopped being for Sabrina and
arted being a way to keep you near me. Why do
u think I sent Lisa Peters to you?"

"Lisa—" It took her a moment to realize he meant the woman whose fortuitous appearance had made it possible for Hope to leave Celebrations and move to the ranch. Understanding dawned. "You mean—"

He shook his head, his eyes filled with wonder. "Hope, you must be the only woman in Texas who wouldn't have seen through that. Lisa's husband has worked for Flying M Enterprises for years. I knew she'd do a good job for you. And at what I'm paying her, believe me, she was glad to do it."

"But last night—" She bit her lip. "I bared my soul and you walked away without a word." Her voice was little more than an agonized whisper. "Why, Trace, if you cared for me at all? I don't understand."

"I didn't understand, either. When I said it was time to be honest, I had something considerably more physical in mind." He touched her chin gently to tilt her face up. "Honey, you scared the hell out of me. That was the first time anyone ever said they loved me and made me believe it." He bent quickly to drop a soft kiss on her lips. "Sabrina once accused me of not believing in love. I denied it, but that was a knee-jerk reaction, because she was right. It took you, my loving and giving Friday's Child, to teach me that." He grinned. "Say it again."

She licked her lips, overcome by shyness. "I . . . love you."

"Again."

"I love you." It was getting easier.

"Again!"

Laughing and breathless with excitement, she threw back her head and shouted, "I love you!"

And then he'd responded with the words she most
longed to hear. "I love you, too, Hope, more than
ever thought possible. Now, here's what we're
going to do—"

And they did, with a little help from friends in
high places. One of those friends was the judge,
stepping forward now with a smile. "Ladies and
gentlemen," he announced, "it's my privilege to
present Mr. and Mrs. Trace Morgan. Trace, you
may kiss your lovely bride."

Mrs. Casen, the matron of honor, arranged the
bride's train as she turned toward her new husband.
Trace caught her left hand in his and lifted it quickly
to his lips, kissing the plain gold band on the third
finger. "Come here, Mrs. Morgan," he drawled.

She went, throwing her arms around his neck and
rising on tiptoe for his kiss. Behind her, she heard
Mrs. Casen murmur in a teary voice, "Bless you,
children. May you live happily ever after."

Hope knew they had that last part licked.

* * * * * *

Saturday's child works hard for its living...
Look out next month for Jessica Hart's
Working Girl, the latest book in
our exciting series.

HUSBANDS ON HORSEBACK

 DIANA PALMER
Paper Husband

MARGARET WAY
Bride in Waiting

Two original stories from two of romance's best-loved authors,
combined in one sensational Harlequin Romance novel.

From the Outback of Australia to Texas soil we
follow the stories of two irresistible men—ranchers
used to wild living, men of whom legends are made.
Now, finally, they're about to meet their match!

Available at your favorite retail outlet.

Harlequin Romance ®

brings you

How the West was Wooed!

We've rounded up twelve of our most popular authors and the result is a whole year of romance, Western-style. Every month we'll be bringing you a spirited, independent woman whose heart is about to be lassoed by a rugged, handsome, one-hundred-percent cowboy! Watch for...

Available wherever Harlequin books are sold.

Look us up on-line at: http://www.romance.net

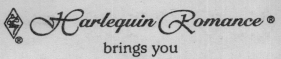
Harlequin Romance ®

brings you

HOLDING OUT FOR A
HERO ★

Some men are worth waiting for!

Every month for a whole year Harlequin Romance will be bringing you some of the world's most eligibl men in our special **Holding Out for a Hero** miniseries. They're handsome, they're charming but best of all, they're single! Twelve lucky women are about to discover that finding Mr. Right is not a problem—it's holding on to him!

Watch for:

#3430 *THE BACHELOR CHASE*
by Emma Richmond

Available in October wherever Harlequin books are sold.

HOFH-

V®

Don't miss these Harlequin favorites by some of our most
distinguished authors!
And now, you can receive a discount by ordering two or more title

HT #25663	THE LAWMAN by Vicki Lewis Thompson	$3.25 U.S.☐/$3.75 CAN.
HP #11788	THE SISTER SWAP by Susan Napier	$3.25 U.S.☐/$3.75 CAN.
HR #03293	THE MAN WHO CAME FOR CHRISTMAS by Bethany Campbell	$2.99 U.S.☐/$3.50 CAN.
HS #70667	FATHERS & OTHER STRANGERS by Evelyn Crowe	$3.75 U.S.☐/$4.25 CAN.
HI #22198	MURDER BY THE BOOK by Margaret St. George	$2.89 ☐
HAR #16520	THE ADVENTURESS by M.J. Rodgers	$3.50 U.S.☐/$3.99 CAN.
HH #28885	DESERT ROGUE by Erin Yorke	$4.50 U.S.☐/$4.99 CAN.

(limited quantities available on certain titles)

	AMOUNT	$
DEDUCT:	**10% DISCOUNT FOR 2+ BOOKS**	$
ADD:	**POSTAGE & HANDLING**	$
	($1.00 for one book, 50¢ for each additional)	
	APPLICABLE TAXES**	$_____
	TOTAL PAYABLE	$_____
	(check or money order—please do not send cash)	

To order, complete this form and send it, along with a check or money order for
total above, payable to Harlequin Books, to: **In the U.S.:** 3010 Walden Aven
P.O. Box 9047, Buffalo, NY 14269-9047; **In Canada:** P.O. Box 613, Fort Erie, Onta
L2A 5X3.

Name: _____

Address: _____ City: _____

State/Prov.: _____ Zip/Postal Code: _____

**New York residents remit applicable sales taxes.
Canadian residents remit applicable GST and provincial taxes.   HBACK-

Look us up on-line at: http://www.romance.net